HIT 149

THE HIT SERIES
BOOK ONE

NEW YORK TIMES BESTSELLER

MARGARET MCHEYZER

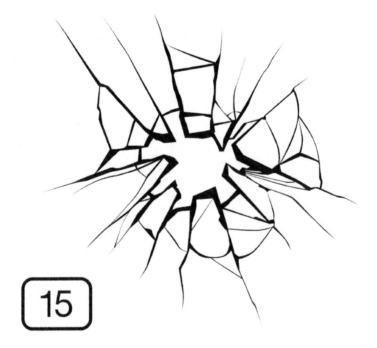

15

HIT 149

The one thing you need to know about me is I've never been a damsel in distress.

Arrogant.

Antihero.

Assassin.

I may be a woman but I'm lethal. My code-name is 15.

The day I turned fifteen was when my life changed forever.

Ronan Murphy sent his men to tear me away from my home by using any force necessary. For survival I put a bullet in their head, but not before they wreaked permanent destruction.

From that day on, I was eternally changed.

Fast forward to my twenty-eighth birthday, where I gave myself the ultimate present... I ended Ronan Murphy's life.

To celebrate, I was on the prowl for a one-night stand.

I met *him* at a bar.

He's strong and sexy.

We hit it off immediately.

He's name was Ben Pearson.

Ben was exactly what I needed to scratch my itch...until he told me he's the police chief in Bankstown Creek, the town I was taken from.

So, I did the only thing I could, I left.

I never wanted to see him again; obviously it's too dangerous for me. My life doesn't need that level of complication.

I would've stayed gone, but now I've been hired for a new job. A hit on a cop - *Ben Pearson*.

I'm to return to my hometown and assassinate him. Problem is, I'm not sure I can.

May your inner assassin take no hostages when she needs to kick ass.

PROLOGUE

I'm a monster.

I sink to the ground and huddle into myself. *What have I done?* My stomach roils with uncertainty as I realize what I was forced to do.

It doesn't matter what I say or do. Everyone will see me as a fifteen-year-old killer. But I had to. I was forced to do what I did, because I know what would have happened to me if they took me.

I lift my chin to stare at the car on the shoulder. Nox and Damon are both dead. Bullets to the backs of their heads. Quick and easy. My only regret is that I didn't do it earlier...before they killed my father.

I find myself on my feet, walking toward the car. I look at the bloody mess and try to feel something. But I can't. They deserved it. They killed my father and tried to kidnap me.

My jaw is aching with tension, and my heartbeat is pounding in my chest. I close my eyes for a moment to regroup and take a few deep breaths to center myself. "It'll be okay, Anna," I whisper to myself. My throat constricts as my mind races through every possibility. If I stay, I'm going to find myself up on charges and in prison. *I killed two people.*

I have to run. There are no other options.

The night is pitch-black, cloudy, with no stars or moon in the sky. "Dad, what do I do?" I whisper before I break down in soul-crushing grief. I give myself a moment to try and clear my foggy thoughts. Dad wouldn't want me to stay here. He'd want me to escape and start a new life.

I take a moment before finally deciding what I'm going to do. I reach the car and rifle through Damon's and Nox's pockets. Luckily, I end up with a wad of cash between the two of them. This will only be enough to last me a month if I'm smart with it. I need to go somewhere far away and figure out what I'm going to do.

Opening the trunk of the car, I find two more guns, rope, tape, and a black backpack containing a dark sweater and hunting knife, and a sheet of plastic. I pull on the sweater and use the hood to cover my head, tucking the hunting knife into the back of my pants and leaving the plastic folded in the backpack. The guns are fully loaded, their serial numbers filed off—fully untraceable. "Assholes," I whisper as I shake my head.

I close the trunk lid and squat beside the car. I count out the cash quickly, open the backpack and stuff it down the bottom, making sure I keep a small amount on me so I can pay for things along the way.

The sick lump sitting in my throat is growing by the moment, and I need to get away from here before a car comes by and sees the mess I've left. There's one more thing I need to do before I leave. I open the passenger door and take Damon's phone out of the center console.

Breathe, Anna, breathe. Dad always taught me to breathe through difficult situations.

I close my eyes and regain my composure. I swallow the tremor in my throat and open my eyes. I make the call.

"Did you get her?"

I pause as heat rises through my body. Blood rushes to my ears with a pounding echo as I struggle to hold onto my emotions. "I'm coming for you."

"What the—"

I hang up, drop the phone beside the car and stomp on it.

My mind is made up. I'll find him, and I'll kill him.

His life will be in my hands, and I'll end it. He gave the order to kill my father and kidnap me. For that he's going to pay.

CHAPTER ONE

—— • ——

THIRTEEN YEARS LATER

My pulse quickens as I look through the scope of my modified sniper rifle. Lying on the roof of this high-rise building, I run through all the variables involved in this hit.

Excitement vibrates through every fiber of my being. *I need this one.* I compose myself as I prepare for what's about to happen. Over the years, I've honed my skills, perfecting them for this very moment.

I look through the scope and see my target approaching, three miles out. I take several deep breaths to calm myself. I can't get this wrong because it's too personal to fail.

I open my eyes and steady my finger over the trigger. So many things can go wrong, but I've been doing this for years and I'm prepared for every possible outcome. I insert my Bluetooth earpiece, dial my phone, and watch as the target speeds toward me.

He becomes crystal clear through my scope, as if he's right in front of me. "What?" Ronan answers as he sits in the back seat and casually turns to look out the window.

"You won't escape me, Ronan."

Sheer terror washes over him. "Turn the car around!" he yells at his driver.

I smirk as I watch him scuttle toward the middle of the back seat in an attempt to duck for cover. "That won't save you." I depress the trigger and hear the lovely sound of the bullet scraping through the chamber. Part of me is worried I'm off on my calculations, but when I see the bullet break the glass of the car and Ronan's head explode toward the rear window, I know I've annihilated my target. "I love you, Dad," I whisper. I've now taken my vengeance for my father's death.

I've carried the burden of Ronan Murphy for thirteen years. I've felt nothing but hatred and venom for him, but he's been in hiding for many years. I lower my head to the ground as an overwhelming warmth radiates through my body. I've wanted this for so long, and now that it's all over, it feels almost surreal. *I did it.* I finally ended the life of the man who ordered my father killed and changed the trajectory of my life forever.

I lay on the rooftop for what feels like hours, watching the aftermath of my kill and allowing the euphoric sensation of revenge to sweep over me. Today is the best day of my life. Not only is it my twenty-eighth birthday, but I finally killed Ronan Murphy. My phone dings and I touch the earpiece. "Yeah."

"How did that feel?" Agent asks.

I roll onto my back and stare up at the crystal-clear sky. Smiling, I relax my hands on my stomach. "I'm kind of lost for words," I say.

"You? The great 15, lost for words? In all the years I've worked for you, I've never known you to *be lost for words*," Agent playfully mocks me. "I bet it felt good though. Tell me it felt good, right?"

I keep staring up at the sky and smile slightly. "He got what he deserved."

Agent snickers into the phone. "Well, I think his car has lost most of its value, especially now there's blood and brains splattered everywhere. I wouldn't want to be the one to clean that up."

"You're a sick bastard," I say as I smile.

"Says the world's deadliest assassin."

I push up off the rooftop and begin to disassemble the sniper rifle. "I'm sure you have work to do." I press my phone disconnecting the call. Once my rifle has been packed away, I take the duffel bag and make my way down from the top of the building. I make sure to pull my hood up and my cap down, lowering my chin so my face can't be caught on any security cameras. Once in the rental car, I head back to the parking garage and take the duffel bag out of the rental and place it in the trunk of my personal car. I take the cleaning fluid and rags out of my car. I carefully wipe everything down before calling Agent to arrange the return of the rental. I step back and look around the garage again before calling Agent. "The car is ready to go."

"Leave the key in the normal spot, and I'll have it taken care of."

I hang up, check to make sure I'm not being watched, and slide the key and fob into the back of the wheel cavity. I slide into the driver's seat of my car and make my way to the hotel.

When I return to the hotel parking lot, I lock my car. I head up to my room, scan my card over the black wall pad, and walk into the spacious suite. I know I have to leave early in the morning, but for tonight, I need to take a step back, unwind and enjoy myself. It's my birthday, after all.

Standing in front of the mirror, I pull my nearly black hair back into a ponytail and apply a layer of lipstick. I take a step back and scan my appearance. The tight red dress accentuates every single one of my curves, from my breasts to my hips. I'm on a mission tonight. I need to find a guy, get laid, and leave before he asks for my number.

Luckily, I've worked in this city a number of times and I know which bars have the type of men I like. I slip my feet into my black heels and turn to look at my reflection from the side. My butt looks damn hot in this figure-hugging dress. Yep, tonight's going to be a good night.

I drive down to the main street and luckily find a parking space not too far from the Lotus Gold Bar. Immediately, I turn heads as I stroll on the sidewalk with my chin high and my shoulders back. I walk into the establishment and head over to the bar, where there are several available seats. Two men positioned on the opposite end of the bar talk between themselves, though both sets of eyes are focused on me. The one with blond hair picks up his drink and waltzes over to me. "Hi, what can I get you?" the female bartender asks. She takes a quick glance at the man who's going to attempt to pick me up.

He takes a black credit card out of his wallet, places it on the bar and slides it toward the bartender. "The lady will have whatever she wants," he says in a tone I can only describe as nails down a chalkboard—irritating.

The bartender looks toward me and raises her brows. "Jack neat please." She flicks her gaze over to the guy again, waiting around to see if I need help. I smile and wink silently telling her, *I've got this*.

"Sure." She turns her back for a moment to pour my drink.

"Hi," the guy says.

I slowly turn my neck and inhale sharply. "No," I finally say.

"What?" His perky smile falters. "I only said hello. The least you can do is say thank you for buying you a drink."

Visibly I drop my eyes to scan his body and click my tongue to the roof of my mouth. He puffs out his chest and stands taller as I lift my gaze to stare into his eyes. I hold the penetrating look for a long moment. The bartender returns and places the glass down on a napkin beside my hand. I've yet to say anything in reply to the guy. I can see her out of my peripheral vision. She appears confused. I take the drink and throw it back in one motion and turn to the bartender. "Another." I slide the guy's card closer to her. "Take an extra twenty for yourself."

"Thank you," she says with a chirp in her voice.

"So, are you going to thank me now?"

I wet and nibble my lower lip, waiting for the bartender to return with my second drink. The moment she does, I down it in one go again. She places the slip in front of the guy for him to sign. I wait until he's done and arch a brow at him again. "You can go now." I shoo him away with a flick of my hand.

His shoulders stiffen and his fingers flex. "What? I bought you two drinks, and gave her a twenty-dollar tip," he says through gritted teeth.

"That sounds like a *you* problem, doesn't it?" I casually look around the bar for the man I'll be allowing to ravage me tonight. No one's caught my eye yet. The night is still young, I guess.

The guy steps closer to me and pushes his chest out in an attempt to intimidate me. "The least you can do is tell me your name."

Casually, I turn and flutter my lashes at him, drawing him in with a false hope. "Come here." I curl my finger at him.

He looks back to his friend and gives him a knowing nod. This guy isn't worth my time, but he also needs to know not to treat women the way he's treated me. "Yeah, baby." He places his hands on my thighs and tightly squeezes. Leaning into me, he utters, "Want to come back to my place?"

I turn and suck his earlobe into my mouth. His fingers dip into my thighs as he leans right into me. "Do you have all your affairs in order?" I whisper as I push my breasts into him. Anyone looking at us from the outside would think this is an intimate exchange between two people about to leave so they can fuck.

"You gonna ride me until I'm dead, baby?"

He makes me sick with all the *baby* name calling. "Oh, *baby*, I'm going to tie you up..." He takes in a sharp, deep breath. He tries to push between my legs, but I keep them firmly closed. "Then I'm going to tear you apart, starting with your tiny, little dick."

"What the fuck..." He tries to step backward, but I grab his hands and keep them in place on my thighs.

"I asked you if you have your affairs in order?" Panic passes over him. He attempts to pull his hands away, but I tighten mine around his wrists. He looks over to his friend, silently begging him to help. "Next time you buy a woman a drink, do it because you want to, not because you expect a God damned thing from her. Do I make myself clear?" He mashes his lips together but finally nods. "Good. Now go back to your friend." I release his hands and as he scuttles away, I say, "Have a good night." I keep my focus on him and smirk as he hightails it out of the bar without even stopping to collect his friend.

"Can I get you another drink?" the bartender asks.

"Thank you," I say with a smile.

She pours me another and slides it across the counter. "I have to say," she says with a slight shake of her head. "That was intense. I've never seen a man leave that quickly before. What did you say to him?"

I smirk as I lift my third bourbon and sip on it. "I told him I'd tie him up and tear him apart."

The bartender blinks rapidly and tilts her head to the side. "Huh, maybe next time I'll try that." She smiles and nods. She thinks I was joking.

I stand from the barstool and lift my bourbon. "Say it with conviction and they'll leave you alone."

"Conviction, you say?"

"As long as you mean what you say, and you say what you mean." Her smile is wide but quickly tightens when she thinks about my words. I open my clutch and take out a twenty.

She shakes her hand to wave the money away. "I like the way you handled him. It's on the house."

"Thank you." I tuck the twenty back into my clutch and walk toward the back of the bar where there are armchairs and sofas under soft lighting. I sit and scan the room, waiting for the type of man I usually prefer to walk in. This may only be for one night, but I'm not going to settle. I'm particular, and only a certain type of man will do.

As I look around the bar, I'm a moment away from abandoning my hunt when *he* catches my attention. My heartbeat quickens, my stomach flip-flops, and my mouth dries out. He's tall, taller than I am, with broad shoulders and muscles that strain beneath his button-up dress shirt. He's holding a glass and speaking with another man of similar height. My one-night stand is focused on his conversation with the other guy. *Excellent. This gives me time to observe him.*

A beautiful, petite woman approaches them, and I narrow my eyes as my jaw clenches. Thankfully, the other guy wraps his arm around her waist and kisses her temple before returning his attention to my one-night stand. The other guy flicks his gaze around the bar as he laughs at something my one-nighter says and sees me staring at them. The corner of his mouth lifts, and he juts his chin toward me.

The other guy turns his head to look. He straightens his shoulders, lifts his chin and saunters toward me. Without saying a word, he stands beside me. He eyes the now-empty glass I'm nursing. "What are you drinking?"

"Bourbon, neat," I reply.

Wordlessly he heads over to the bar, orders two drinks and returns with them. He hands one to me, but I wasn't born yesterday. Just because I'm going to fuck him, it doesn't mean I trust him. "What?" he asks when I don't lift the glass to my lips.

"Have a sip." I offer it to him.

"You watched me walk over to the bar and order it, then slide it off the bar and carry it over here." I smirk as I arch a brow while still holding the glass out to him. He quickly relents, reaches for my glass and takes a sip. "Better?"

"Now, sip yours too." I clasp the glass and wait for him to have a drink of his.

"You're either paranoid..."

"Or I'm cautious. I prefer to go with a healthy suspicion of anyone I don't know."

A small smirk appears from behind the glass he's lifted to his mouth. "I get the sense you don't trust a lot of people."

"I trust myself."

"You can trust me not to drug you." I chuckle aloud. "What?"

"Makes me wonder if your words have multiple meanings."

He glances down at his now empty glass. He takes in a long, slow breath before sitting back and relaxing against the sofa. "I have to say, I haven't seen you here before."

"Passing through." So, he lives here.

"Do you have a name, or should I call you..." he pauses and taps his fingers on his knee. "Miss Vigilant?"

"Vigilant or vigilante?"

"You're way too beautiful to be a vigilante," he says.

"Why can't I be both? A beautiful vigilante." I shrug, liking that image for myself, although it's a new one for me.

"Well." He holds his hand out for me to shake. This is the moment I'll know exactly the type of person he is. I reach for his hand, dreading this to my very core. I hold my breath as I wrap my fingers around his to shake his hand. Thankfully, I don't sense that all-encompassing feeling of doom and dread when I take his hand. The venom sting that twists my gut and blankets me in icy cold goose bumps when I touch a dangerous person, almost like a sixth sense that has served me well over the years. It's never let me down. "Ben Pearson."

"Anna Moore," I respond.

His thumb strokes the skin on the back of my hand. "Exactly how *vigilant* are you, Anna Moore?"

Without moving my head, I lower my eyes to look at where our hands are joined together. I lean in and whisper, "Perhaps I should show you in private, *Ben Pearson*."

He doesn't release my hand as he stands and pulls me up with him. "My hotel is close by." My step falters and I don't follow him. Something feels slightly off, which is bizarre because I didn't get any kind of feeling from him. "What is it?"

"You said you haven't seen me here before. Why would you be in a hotel if you're a regular here?"

"Wow, you really *are* suspicious." He drops my hand and runs his over his angular jaw. "My sister lives here, and I regularly visit her. Come on." Ben reaches for my hand again. "I'll introduce you."

"No, thank you." I wave my hand at him. "Besides, it's not like I can't hurt you with my bare hands if you try anything you shouldn't."

Ben throws his head back and laughs, as if I'm joking. *If only he knew.* He takes his wallet out of his back pocket, and removes the card key to his room. "I'm going to say goodbye to my sister. Here." He thrusts the key toward me. "Hilton. Room two-oh-one." I hesitate for a split second, not taking the key. "Unless you want to come with me."

He's mistaken my delay for worry. No, this is something bigger than he thinks. I take the key and slide it into my purse. "Don't take too long, or I'll start without you."

Ben wraps his arm around me and draws me close to his body. His excitement is obvious. "Don't you dare," he whispers.

I walk out of the bar and head toward my car. He's in room 201, it has to be a coincidence that Ronan Murphy was my two-hundred and first kill today. My mind reels with every possible connection between Ben and Ronan Murphy. As I pull into a parking facility close to his hotel, I sit in my car, trying to shut my brain off. But something keeps dragging my mind back to the correlating numbers. Could there be a significance?

I push those thoughts to the back of my mind, reach for my clutch, and check that I have condoms with me before I exit my car and head up to his room. I check my phone to find I've been stuck in my head for a good ten minutes. "Damn," I murmur to myself. That's ten minutes of Ben's head between my thighs I've missed out on.

I use the key Ben gave me to open the hotel room door. As it closes behind me, I'm pushed up against the wall. His lips are all over me as his hands roam my body. His body has mine pinned up against the door. I tear at his shirt, disregarding the buttons as they fly off in different directions.

This is raw. Needy...hot. We're tearing at each other's clothes, making quick work of getting them off.

"You're nothing like any woman I've ever met before," he whispers as he cups the back of my thigh and wraps it around his hip.

Ben's about to push into me. "Wait, you need a condom," I say breathlessly.

He leans his forehead against mine, taking a moment to catch his breath. "Fuck," he whispers with resignation.

"You'd think you'd be prepared," I tease. "Luckily I am." I eye my clutch that's on the floor beneath my dress.

Ben releases my leg and steps back as he scrubs his hand over his face. "I'm impressed by how progressive you are."

I scoot my dress out of the way and pick my clutch up. Opening it, I take out one of the condoms and tear it out of the foil packet. "If you think me carrying a condom is progressive, wait until I fuck you."

Ben is eagerly standing near the bed, his cock rock-hard. "Jesus," he murmurs as I wrap my fingers around it with confidence and slowly move my hand up and down the shaft. His eyes roll back as he allows his chin to lift. I slide the condom on, and while my mouth is on his, I walk him backward toward the bed. When I find resistance, I push him down and climb on top of him. I line us up and sink down, both of us exhale with a desperate pleasure. He grabs my hips and flexes his fingers as I rotate my hips. "Anna." His breath is ragged and dense. But in one movement, he has me on my back, forcing me to wrap my legs around his hips. "You feel so good."

"Shut up and fuck me harder," I say, then pull his head down to kiss me.

It only takes him a few moments of ramming into me before I'm on the edge of my own release. I lower my hand between us, but he smacks it away and rubs his thumb against my clit. "Get your hand away. This is my job."

I stretch my arms over my head, appreciating his touch. Heat rises through me quickly, and I find myself on the verge of an orgasm. "I'm coming." My hips move with his. "Keep doing that." I erupt around his cock while he growls from deep inside his chest. A strained moan bursts through him as he comes undone.

Ben props himself up on his elbows and gently kisses me. I push him off and head into the bathroom to clean myself. I look in the mirror and smile at my messy hair and puffy lips from kissing him so hard. I take in a deep breath and pull my shoulders back. I want round two before I leave.

I open the door and Ben stands from the bed to head into the bathroom. I cast a cheeky look up and down his body. "You look good enough to do that again."

He stops walking and laces his fingers through my hair. Ben lowers and kisses me with passionate heat. "Give me half an hour and we'll go again," he murmurs against my lips.

"Half an hour? Pffft." I step away from him, shaking my head.

"Hey, it's only half an hour I need," he says with sarcasm. "Maybe forty-five minutes," he mumbles as he slowly closes the door to the bathroom. "An hour tops."

Laughing, I slide into bed and bring the covers up over my body. In all his glory, he saunters back into the room and gets in the bed beside me. "An hour? Sheesh." I playfully cringe. "Do I really have to wait that long?" I tease.

He lies on his side as I flip myself over on my stomach. "Tell me about yourself, Anna." *Ugh, no thank you.* "Where are you from?"

"Florida," I reply, my rehearsed standard answer. Nothing personal needs to be exchanged here, and if I know what's good for me, I should be sliding my dress on and saying thank you on the way out the door. "Tell me something about you."

He begins drawing lazy circles on my back as he stares into my eyes. "My sister and her husband live here and I have another sister who lives in New York City with her husband."

"Why are you staying in a hotel instead of staying with your sister?"

He moves himself over and kisses my shoulder. "Frankly, because I don't want to."

"So, there's you and two sisters. No brothers?" He shakes his head as he peppers slow kisses over my shoulder and neck. "What do you do?"

"I manage people in a tiny town."

"Where is this tiny town?" I lean over and place a kiss on his mouth. "Do tiny towns still exist?"

"They do where I come from. I live in Minnesota."

I momentarily freeze. *Please don't say Bankstown Creek.* I hold onto my resolution as I ask, "Where in Minnesota? I ask because I've been through there a few times."

"What do you do to travel around so much?"

"I'm in human resources..." I pause and smirk internally. "More like headhunting." He's yet to answer what small town he lives in. "Although I'm based in Florida, I travel quite a lot for work." That's not entirely a lie; I do travel a lot for work. Even the headhunting part is true, just not the way he'd interpret it. "Tell me about this small town you live in. Is it one of those places that has a population of five thousand people and everyone knows everyone's business."

Ben chuckles. "Not exactly that small, the population is around thirty thousand people. But I doubt you've heard of it. I live in Bankstown Creek."

My stomach tenses as my breath catches in my throat. "No, I can't say I've heard of it," I say with conviction. "What do you do in Bankstown Creek?" I'm going to have to get out of here. This is too close for me.

"Well, don't get intimidated but..." Intimidated? Me? "I'm the police chief for Bankstown Creek."

Fuck. Manage people, my ass. He's a damn cop.

My mind races with thousands of thoughts. I know everything about Bankstown Creek because that's where I grew up. My dad was the police chief of Bankstown Creek. "What's Bankstown Creek like?" I keep my voice steady, making sure not to show any emotion.

"It's a sleepy town. Not much ever happens there. About fifteen years ago the police chief at the time was murdered. It was terrible."

I swallow the bile sitting at the base of my throat. "Have you lived there all your life?"

"No, not at all. I moved only a few years ago. For the job actually."

There are so many questions I want to ask, especially concerning my dad. "So, it's a quiet town?" I have to get out of here. This is too much of a coincidence for me.

I push the covers off my naked body and slide out of the bed. "What are you doing?" Ben asks as he moves to stand. "Are you okay?" He watches as I pick up my clothes and dress.

"I have to leave early in the morning. Thanks for this. It was what I needed."

Ben lunges toward me. "Wait." He struggles to pull his boxer briefs up as I try to make an escape. "Wait!" He grabs my upper arm, stopping me from leaving. I can easily break out of his grip, but something stops me. I don't want to leave, but it's too risky to stay. "Don't leave. Stay and have dinner with me tomorrow night." There's a crazy spark between us, something I've never felt before. Why do I feel so comfortable around him? It's almost like we were made for one another, like he's my destiny. "You can't tell me you don't feel this." He tightens his grip around my arm and lowers his head to look at where we're joined.

It's impossible to have any type of relationship in my line of work. I can't put a civilian in danger by allowing him into my world. Not to mention

Ben's a fucking cop. I need to raise all of my exterior walls. Scowling, I shrug out of his grip. "You were a fuck. I had an itch, you scratched it."

Ben sucks in a small breath; he visibly swallows as he pulls his shoulders back with an unnatural stiffness. He's hurt, and rightfully so. He shakes his head as he relaxes his body. "I don't think you believe that."

I need to go in for the kill and end this right now before I do something stupid, like stay. "That's the problem." I lift my upper lip on the side in snarkiness. "You have too pretty a face to think." I push past him, open the door and leave. Ugh, I hate that I treated him so badly. He didn't deserve that. But this is a case of self-preservation and it was necessary, because he couldn't survive in my world.

Only hard cases like me can safely live in a world of treachery, violence, and complete darkness.

CHAPTER TWO

The drive back to one of my apartment buildings is long and tedious, mostly because my head has been swimming since my encounter with Ben. There was too much at stake to pursue anything more than one night with him.

An assassin and a cop. Yeah, right. Like that could ever work.

I pack my weapons away as I continue to relive the encounter with Ben. No man has ever affected me the way he did, but we only fucked. So why has he made such an impact on me? I have to push this to the side. I can't let it take over my thoughts.

My phone vibrates on the clean kitchen counter in my restored apartment. There's only ever one person who calls me, so I know he's set up a job interview for me. "Agent," I answer as I walk over to the fridge and take out a bottle of water.

"Did you do anything fun?" he asks in a chirpy voice. I open the lid of the water and drink some, refusing to answer him. "You'd think after getting laid, you'd be happier." I arch a brow and smile but still don't respond. "Fine," he concedes. "Firestone Building at twenty-three hundred."

"Thank you."

"Oh! She speaks. I was wondering if you'd suddenly turned mute."

Smart-ass. I hang up and place my phone on the counter. Agent has been with me since the beginning. There's only a handful of people I trust, and he's one of them, maybe because he knows the consequences if he ever betrays me. I have a few hours to spare before the interview, so I head into the weapons room to do an inventory so I can let Agent know about anything I'm running low on.

Before I know it, I need to get ready for my interview. I look over to my two custom handguns, check them for ammunition, and take them with me before locking the steel-reinforced door to my weapons room. In my bedroom, I lay them on the bed and begin to get ready. I tie my hair back into a tight ponytail and change into black tights, flat black boots, and my black, fitted, long-sleeved t-shirt. I strap my guns to my thighs and take a deep breath before leaving my apartment.

In the underground garage, I take the keys to my Toyota out of the box hanging on the wall that holds the keys for all my vehicles. The Firestone Building is in a shit area of town, and anything else will stick out and become a magnet for trouble.

The drive to the building takes just under an hour, and when I reach the destination, I still have enough time to run the perimeter and set up discreet monitoring equipment. The inside of the building is decrepit and derelict. There are a few homeless people sleeping there so I move them along, making sure they're not caught in the cross fire if my interview goes bad. Innocent civilians are never my target, nor should they be.

I place my earpiece in and tap it to dial Agent. "Are you in place?" His entire demeanor has changed from earlier. He's all business now, ready and waiting for my instructions.

"I am," I reply.

"I've got eyes on the building." I hear him tapping on his keyboard. "There are a few homeless coming toward you, east entrance."

I jog over to the door on the east and stand in the way. "Closed." I point behind the group of five people who attempt to move past me. "We're closed." I stand straighter and peer down at my guns strapped to my thighs.

"We don't want any trouble," one of the men replies as he steps backward.

"Then leave," I warn sternly.

"Yes, ma'am." He drops his chin while nodding, refusing to look at me. They turn away to leave.

I stand watching them, in case they attempt to sneak in. They round the corner of the building, and I wait for Agent. "They're gone," he says.

"Good."

Job interviews can be intense. It's when all my senses need to be sharp so I know exactly what's happening. One small mistake can lead to death. Unless it's me putting a bullet between someone's eyes, I'm not keen on complications.

"Two cars approaching. Both are black SUVs," Agent relays the information. "Approaching from the north."

I walk out of the building to wait for my potential employer. "Are we still clear?"

"Wait, there's another car approaching from the south."

The two SUVs stop close to me. It takes another moment before the front passenger door of the first SUV opens. The lights from the SUVs are still on, giving them a clear view of me. The guy is dressed in a suit with his hair slicked back. *Can he be any more of a cliché?* He scans the surroundings, then walks around to open the back door behind the driver.

"They're remaining firm in place," Agent says about the other car that must be here for backup.

I take a deep breath as I watch what's happening with the SUVs. I need to be prepared for whatever unfolds here. From the back, I see an older man, possibly in his late fifties, emerge from the car. He throws his cigarette to the ground and stomps it out as he buttons his suit jacket and adjusts his cuffs. He carefully looks around until he sees me.

"They haven't left the car."

Another man exits the second SUV and walks to stand in front of the main guy. The main guy says something to the other two before the three of them approach me. "Who are you?" the first guy says to me as he stands in front of the client.

I look over his shoulder to the client, then back to him. He carefully draws his gaze down my body, and snickers when his gaze lands on my guns. I arch a brow at him but quickly survey the environment we're in. "Target." I hold my hand out for the file.

"I asked who the fuck you are?" He pulls his shoulders back and lifts his chin, attempting to be menacing.

I move my hands over my guns, ready for whatever is going to happen.

"The front doors are opening," Agent says. "No one's leaving the car though."

I look at the client and take in a sharp breath. "Are you here for business, or are you here for a damned playdate?" I pause long enough to make my point. "Target profile." I extend my hand for a second time.

"She's a fucking joke," the guy standing beside the client says.

"Get back in the car. This is a waste of time," the first guy says.

The main guy isn't so sure about leaving yet. "If she's a killer then I'll eat a fucking bullet," the guy in the back says.

Without missing a heartbeat, my guns are in my hands and I've put a bullet through his mouth. The first guy startles and the main guy becomes rigid but quickly snaps into gear and has his gun out aiming at me.

"Two coming in from behind you," Agent says.

"Drones," I say as I position myself with guns pointing steadily toward the people in front of me.

"On it." I hear Agent typing, then the whirl of my drones hovering.

"What the fuck is that?" the client asks as he looks around.

"Are we doing business, or not?"

"We're good back here," Agent says.

A drone lowers behind them, essentially trapping them where they are. The main guy looks around, then smirks. He steps forward and places his hand on the first guy. "Enough," he says. I haven't moved, and I'm prepared to put a bullet in his head too. His wild eyes are telling me he's not prepared to holster his weapons. "Enough," the client repeats slower. The other guy snarls and while maintaining eye contact, he holsters his gun. I keep mine trained on him. The client steps forward and holds his hands up to me. "We're good."

"They're back in the car," Agent says.

"Keep the drones," I reply as I keep my hard stare on the client. "Are you ready to do business now?"

He steps forward with his hands still up. "I'm sorry about that." He slowly lowers his hands and points behind him. "He was disrespectful, and for that I apologize." He slowly shoves his hand into his pocket, but I don't trust this fucker, so I keep one of my guns trained on him and the other gun pointed toward the other asshole. The drone hovers behind, ready to deploy more gunfire if needed. "Your retainer fee of one million has been wired to this account." He holds a paper out toward me. "The other million will be wired to the same account once you've completed the job."

Unrelenting, I don't lower my weapons. "Two million is my fee when I'm not disrespected. My fee has increased to three million. Two now, and one upon completion."

The client turns to the one remaining and shakes his head. He reaches into his suit jacket pocket and retrieves his phone. His jaw jumps as he glares at his phone and shakes his head again, before lifting it to look at me, then lowers his chin once again. "I could use you on my staff."

My lip curls as I snicker to myself. "If the next words that leave your mouth aren't I've transferred the money into your account, we're done here." I stare at him without emotion. "I'll keep the retainer and you can leave."

He keeps a firm eye on me for a moment, but I'm unwavering; I'll shoot him between the eyes and walk away without another thought. He twists his mouth as he runs his tongue over his teeth before looking down at his phone. "Two million has been transferred, and the remainder will be done upon completion of the job."

"Check," I say to Agent as I keep my guns trained on the client and the other jackass.

"It's come through," Agent responds.

"Target," I coldly say to the client.

He flicks his hand toward the other guy who opens the back door of the second SUV and retrieves a large envelope. He walks over to hand it to me, but I flick my gaze to the ground in front of me as I refuse to lower my weapons. "There." He tosses it to my feet. "Leave," I instruct them all.

"When will my problem be handled?" the client asks with anticipation.

"When it's done, you'll know."

"This isn't the way business is done." He looks at the file at my feet.

"This is the way *I* do business."

He runs his hands through his hair, then finally nods. He turns to the first guy and makes a circular movement with his fingertip. They get into their SUVs and begin to pull away. "Watch them," I say to Agent.

"The car from the north has already left, but I have a drone following them to make sure they don't double back."

My guns are still drawn and I'm watching them intently. At any moment they could come at me and try to run me down, though if they did that, they'd be dead and I'd be two million richer for a job I didn't need to complete. *That wouldn't be the first time.* I chuckle to myself.

I wait for Agent's confirmation that they've left before I holster my weapons and pick up the file. I look over at the guy lying on the ground and shake my head. Walking out to my car, I slide in and place the file beside me. "Am I clear?" I ask from my idling car.

"Yeah, they're gone. Take the backup route and you won't cross paths with them."

I leave my earpiece in as I navigate my way back home. I pull into my parking garage and take the file with me as I make my way up to my apartment. I throw the file on the kitchen counter before I head into the weapons room and put my guns away.

I step back and double-check that my guns are all in place before closing the door. I head into the kitchen to grab some water before I have a shower and go to bed. The file sits on my kitchen counter, but I'm not interested in looking at it tonight. I'll get to it when I wake up.

I'm done for the day.

CHAPTER THREE

O pening my eyes, I take a breath before I push the covers back and sit up. I scrub my hand over my eyes and yawn. Rolling my head from side to side, I twist my neck to hear and feel the welcome relief of a loud crack.

I have a lot to do today, so I'm quick in the bathroom. Tying my hair back in a high ponytail, I slide on shorts, a sports bra and sports shoes so I can head down to the gym to hit the treadmill and do some weight training.

As usual, time in the gym is accompanied by body aches, sweat, and a feeling of overall satisfaction. My body is a tool, and pushing it is nearly as important to me as target practice. Swiping my water bottle from the floor, I drain it before heading up to my apartment.

My gaze fastens on the file sitting on the kitchen counter beside my phone. A part of me wants to delay this job to teach the client a lesson about fucking me around. However, I'm fully aware that I have a job to do. I slide the file off the counter and go to sit on the armchair in the living room. Looking around, I make a mental note that I really should buy some more furniture. But at the same time, I don't really need anything more than my armchair and a coffee table. I let out a deep sigh as I open the folder.

What? No, wait. This has to be some kind of mistake.

My brows draw together as I stare at the photo. *Ben Pearson.* I lower the photo and lift my chin to look at the exposed brick wall. "This can't be right," I murmur to myself. The client must have the wrong person. The target *can't* be Ben; it has to be someone else. I shake my head as I attempt to dislodge the reality of what I have been hired to do. I don't want to kill Ben. But I have to because that's the job I've taken.

I take several deep breaths to calm my mind. "This is your job." I nod once and pull myself together. He can't be Ben anymore. Now, he's simply a hit. *A target.* I turn the photo of Ben over and open the file again to see what information the client has on him.

I slide a piece of paper from the file and take another deep breath as I shake my head.

Name: Benjamin Adrian Pearson.

Address: 2022 Lionsgate Road, Bankstown Creek, Minnesota.

Occupation: Police Chief, Bankstown Creek Police Department, Minnesota.

My focus is stuck on the address. Lionsgate Road…

I release the paper from my hand, allowing it to slowly glide to the floor. I sit forward in my armchair, lean my elbows on my knees and bring my hands up to cover my face. "What is going on?" A lump of bile sits at the base of my throat as my stomach punishes me with tight spasms. Is this some kind of sick joke?

My chest is tight as I try to wrap my head around the address.

"No," I say as I lift my head and drop my hands. Forcefully, I stand to my feet and head for my phone. I dial Agent.

"15?" I pause, I don't know what to say to him. "Are you hurt?" Agent's voice switches to a more worried tone. "I'll get Doctor."

"No," I say as I regain my train of thought.

"What do you need?"

Ben's picture catches my attention, and I swallow back the hurt pounding in my chest. "Don't book any appointments for the next month."

"Why? Is this new job going to be a problem?"

I wet my lips and gather my thoughts. "There's some extra background work I need to do, so I need the time."

"Okay. I won't take any new work."

I hang up and toss my phone on the counter.

I walk over to the file lying on the floor and look down at the photo and the other papers. I have to do this, or the client will send someone else to kill Ben, and they'll send somebody else after me for blowing the job. I'm not worried about myself as much as I'm worried for Ben.

Truth be told, there was something about Ben, he... I blink several times as I worry my lip between my teeth. I don't know, maybe I felt some kind of connection to him. A wave of agony presses heavily on me as I weigh up all my options. I've always relied on my gut and the feel of ice that crawls through my veins when I meet someone who's dangerous. Ben never gave me that feeling. Why would someone want to kill him?

Moreover, that someone is paying me three million dollars to do it. Something's not adding up, and I have to find out why.

I pick up the photo and the papers and put them together again. I have to figure out what's going on with Ben. I head into my walk-in closet and wheel out my suitcase. I pack enough clothes to last me a week, then head back into my weapons room and pack the guns I usually take wherever I go. Ben will be an easy hit, I can kill him within a moment of getting close to him. That's not what I'm worried about, though. I'm just not sure I *want* to do it.

I head into the bathroom and grab a quick shower while my head swims with the fact that someone wants to kill Ben. I can't imagine why. Maybe it has something to do with his job. He's a police chief, which means a lot of bad things would cross his desk. Perhaps someone needs him out of the way for a particular reason.

This is why I need to get to Bankstown Creek and work out why there's a hit out for Ben. Once I know what's going on, I'll take his life. *I think.*

The drive has been excruciating for me, not because I've been driving for a solid eight hours and I still have more to go before I reach Bankstown Creek, but because there's a range of emotions stirring inside me. Returning to Bankstown Creek isn't something I've ever looked forward to. Especially considering this is where my father was killed.

My eyes are feeling heavy and I know I need to pull over for the night in order to sleep. I approach a turn off from the highway, seeing a sign for a town called Mulberry Point. I take the turn off and follow the signs, hoping to find a hotel for the evening. Somewhere I can lay low for the night and know that no one will recognize me.

I pull over and search for local hotels or even bed and breakfasts. I generally prefer them as opposed to larger chain hotels because Agent can easily break past their firewalls to destroy any evidence of me being there. In my search, I see a small chain hotel called Embassy Suites.

I begin my journey toward Embassy Suites and call Agent. "If you're calling to find out the time, please press one," Agent jokes. "If you'd like to know the movie of the week, please press two."

I smile as I shake my head. "This could be an emergency," I say.

"You're in your car, near some small hick town in the middle of nowhere. If this was an emergency, I'd know about it before you even called. Now, if you want to order pizza, please press three."

"You're an ass," I say.

"If you require a sexy as fuck geek to do some super-awesome computer work, please press four."

"I'll be approaching the Embassy Suites in about ten minutes, wipe me out of their system."

"If you want to know the joke of the week, please press five."

Rolling my eyes, I hang up, not wanting to listen to him anymore. Although it's not that late, I know I'm going to need to be vigilant tomorrow when I reach Bankstown Creek. I pull up to the secure garage and hit the intercom, waiting for someone to respond. "Embassy Suites."

"I'll be a guest in your hotel tonight."

"Thank you, ma'am. Take any spot you find that doesn't have a reserved sign." The door slowly ascends, and my tires screech as I take off into the underground garage. I find the first available spot to park my car. Taking my bag out of the trunk, I walk toward the elevator that takes me up to reception.

The moment I'm in the foyer, I discretely look around to make sure there's no one here to recognize me. Not only that, I need to make sure there are no dangers nearby.

I walk up to the young woman at the front desk. Her eyes take in the suitcase I'm wheeling behind me and she plasters a false smile on her face. "Good evening, ma'am, do you have a reservation with us?" She subtly skims the top half of my body and arches a brow.

Judgmental people can eat a dick.

"No, I don't have a reservation. Do you have any suites available?" I look at her name tag and see that her name is Crystal. She looks like what I expect a Crystal to look like. Long, blonde, perfect hair and fake nails that make a tick-tick sound when she taps on the keyboard.

Crystal looks up and scrunches her mouth. "Um." She glances to someone behind me and giggles like a child.

Annoyed, I turn to see who she's looking at. Two men dressed in sharp suits are waiting to speak with her. I catch one staring at my ass, and the other taking his wedding ring off and shoving it in his pocket. Something seems off about them, like they have the ability to wreak havoc wherever they go. Huffing, I roll my eyes and return my attention to Crystal. I can't help but notice that her reaction to them is a complete contradiction to the way she's treating me. She flutters her lashes a few times at the men behind me. They are too old for her. I catch one of them saying something about a threesome, and it makes my blood boil. Truthfully, I don't give a shit who does what with who, but it's clear they're planning to take advantage of this young woman.

And she's going to let them. She's going to have a broken heart after they use her and leave her—and if she's lucky, nothing worse.

"We do have a vacancy tonight, ma'am," she starts saying. "We have a comfortable room on the second floor."

"Do you have anything higher with a view?"

"Um." Her jaw tenses as she sucks in a deep breath. "We do have the Presidential Suite, but that's two thousand for the night," she says with a slightly elevated voice.

"That'll do."

"But it's two thousand a night," she reminds me as she keeps passing judgement.

The two guys behind me snicker. My appearance must suggest to them that I can't afford a place like this. Maybe my torn jeans, hoody, and running shoes are the giveaway. "Is that all?" I ask as I cringe internally. I pull one of my credit cards out from my back pocket and slide it over to her.

"Oh," she says as she takes the card from me. She signs me in, waits for authorization on the charge, and gives me the black plastic key for the room. "Top floor, room eight."

I take my credit card and the key and begin to walk away. The two guys step forward and ask Crystal about things to do here. She giggles and begins to tell them about a few attractions the town has. As I'm about to leave it alone, one of the guys asks her if she's into group sex.

Not on my watch, buddy. I roll my suitcase back to the reservation desk and stand way too close to the two guys. One of them turns to look at me and smirks. "Maybe we can make it a foursome. I wouldn't mind watching you two go down on each other," he says as he skims my body.

"I'm down for it," the other guy says.

I stand staring at them, refusing to look away. They're both snickering and laughing; I keep my eyes focused on them, completely unrelenting. "I can make you feel real good, sugar." He steps closer and pushes his body into mine.

I've yet to say a word to either of them. I look at Crystal and say, "You're too smart to be nothing more than these guys' fucktoy for the night."

Crystal's smile quickly fades.

"Hey, maybe she's into having fun," the guy closest to me says. "She looks like a good-time girl." He turns to her and asks, "Are you? You're a dirty slut who loves to have every hole filled, don't you?" I run my tongue over my teeth while staring at him. He wraps his arm around my waist and drags me closer to him. He leans into me and whispers, "Maybe you're a dirty whore too."

I look at him from below my lashes and smile sweetly. I place my hand on his chest and step in so our bodies are nearly melting together. I angle into him and lift my hand to play with the hair at the base of his neck. I push my fingers into his hair and move so close, I'm able to suck his earlobe into my mouth. A small groan of want escapes him. "I can be your dirty whore," I whisper.

"You're a bad, bad girl."

"You and your buddy are going to pack your shit and leave right now."

His chuckle is supposed to be evil, but I can hear the fear. "And why's that, sugar?"

"Because I'll gut you from your neck to your limp cock before I cut it off and shove it in your mouth." I drop my hand and wrap it around his crotch. Squeezing, I apply enough pressure to cause him to suck in a deep breath. I step back and keep my eyes on him. "If you think I'm joking, then let me play, *sugar*." I squeeze tighter, causing his eyes to water. "Leave." I drop my hand and step backward, staring at both the guys. "You." I point to Crystal, whose face is now a flaming scarlet. "Don't be a fucking idiot. That's how you can find yourself in dangerous situations, and you deserve more than them." I snarl toward the two idiots.

She lowers her chin and looks down at the computer. While watching the guys, I wheel my suitcase back toward the elevator. Once up in the room, my phone pings and I look at it. "Well, that was interesting," Agent says. "I'm watching them just to make sure they don't come knocking on your door."

"Are they giving Crystal a hard time?"

"Actually, they both left about thirty seconds after you did. They've gone back up to their rooms." He clicks on the keyboard, and I toe off my shoes and fall onto the bed, trying to relax. "I've erased all footage of you everywhere."

"Good, keep me up to date if those assholes make any move other than leaving."

"They might stay in their room, terrified of you."

"They better leave or I'll pay them a visit." I close my eyes and rub at the tension across the tops of my eyebrows.

"Have I ever told you, you can be terrifying?"

"I kill people for a living, I should *hope* I can be terrifying."

"You know, I have to say, it's not the killing. It's when you torture people that makes my skin crawl."

I smile to myself. "Don't do anything that warrants me torturing you, and you're safe."

Agent takes in a sharp breath. "Shit."

I don't like the tone of his voice. I sit up in bed and reach for my shoes. "What?"

"They're heading back to the front desk. Neither look happy."

"Fuck," I grumble as I tie my shoes, then heave my suitcase up on the bed. Opening it, I search for my guns and tuck them into the back of my jeans, then pull my top down to conceal them. I shove my key in my pocket and head out of the door within a few seconds. "What are they doing?"

"They're down at reception and they look like they're getting loud."

I transfer the call from my phone over to my earpiece and take off. I take the stairs instead of waiting for the elevator. Once I reach the foyer, I close my eyes and take a deep breath. "What's happening?"

"They're hanging back because someone approached the counter where the girl is." I open the door and look around. "You're good," Agent gives me the all clear.

Quietly, I sneak up on the guys and push in between them. "What the fuck?" one guy says as he looks over to me.

"I told you to leave."

They both straighten and become rigid. "No bitch is going to tell us what to do," one says.

"Why do you always find trouble wherever you go?" Agent asks.

"I suggest you both leave. Right now."

They look to each other and smirk. The less vocal of the two opens his suit jacket to show me a gun. "We'll leave, but we want to have some fun first. Care to join us?"

"Fuck, these guys are gonna get themselves killed," Agent says as he watches us remotely.

I eye the gun and snicker while shaking my head. They have no idea who they're dealing with. "You sure you want to do this?" I ask as I exhale an exasperated groan.

He looks me over again and licks his lips. "We've had our fair share of *fun* with little girls like you before."

I glance over at Crystal, who's watching us from behind the counter. "She's called the police," Agent says. I slightly shake my head for him to kill the call out. "On it." He works his hacking magic as he types on the keyboard. "It's done."

"Boys, if you want to party, then let's party." I look at the first guy, then smile at the second. "But I'm telling you right now, you don't want to do this."

"The hell we don't. It's either you or her."

The other one laughs. "Maybe it'll be you *then* her."

"I'll tell you what, if you can walk after I'm done with you, then you can have her." I jut my head to the side to indicate Crystal. I hear Agent laugh through the earpiece.

"Then let's take it back to your room."

"I'm shy. Let's go to your room instead," I say to the guy with the gun.

He grabs me by my upper arm and leads me toward the elevator. My skin prickles when he touches me, I already know this guy is evil as fuck. "You know you can't kill them, right?" Agent asks casually. I roll my eyes as I discreetly shake my head. "Well, technically you can, but you shouldn't."

"Bareback with this one. Teach her a lesson," one says to the other as we wait for the elevator. "I want her ass."

"These guys can't be serious. Who talks like that?" Agent asks. "Low-level thugs who think they're important, that's who," Agent answers his own question.

The elevator door opens and they shove me in from behind. I quickly put my back against the elevator wall so they can't feel my guns. The elevator climbs and these two are grinning, exchanging knowing looks. Once the door opens again, the guy takes his gun out, wraps his fingers tight around the top of my arm and drags me along as he points the gun into my side. "My gun is going to be wedged in your mouth while we fuck you," he whispers.

Agent snickers. The other guy jogs ahead to open the door and looks down the corridor to make sure they're not seen. The other pushes me into the room and grabs me around the throat, tightening his grip on me. "You stupid fucking slut. You should've let us have the other cunt." He pushes me up against the back of the now-closed door.

"Maybe you *should* kill them," Agent says.

Closing my eyes for a few seconds gives me enough time to gain my composure and assess what's happening. These guys think they can mess around with me, but they have no idea I'm Satan. I reach around behind me, and grab both my guns, bringing them up and pointing them directly at the guy with his hands around my neck. One gun is pointed at his chest, the other at his crotch. His fingers loosen around my throat as he sucks in a ragged breath. "Where did you say you're going to put that gun while you fuck me?"

"What the fuck?" the other guy says as he reaches for his gun.

The guy in front of me takes a hesitant step back, giving me the leverage I need. I point one gun to his head, and the other gun points at the other guy's head. "Throw them on the floor." I pointedly look to their guns.

With shaking hands, they toss the guns to the floor. "Who are you?"

"You guys are fucking wimps," I say as I shake my head. "You talk the talk, but you crumble like cocksuckers. Jesus," I say with mirth. This really is fun for me.

"Oh my God, they're pussies," Agent says.

"Step back." I walk toward them, pushing them away from the guns on the floor.

"Seriously, you've already disarmed them? This has got to be some kind of record, 15."

I scoot the guns under the bed with my foot while I still have mine pointed at them. "Who do you work for?" I ask as I sit on the edge of the bed.

"What? We don't work for anyone," one says.

"At this stage I want you to kill them for being dumb-asses," Agent says.

I flick my gaze between the two of them and sigh, aggravated at having to repeat myself. "Who do you work for?" They look to each other and purse their lips together. "I'll make it easy for you. The first one to speak, lives." I lift the guns higher pointing them at their heads again.

Fear enshrouds them both. All the blood drains out of their faces, leaving them pale while their breath hitches. "Ruben Hall," one says.

I've done a couple of jobs for Ruben, and he knows who I am. "Patch him in," I say to Agent.

The two thugs look at each other, unaware of who I'm talking to. "Dialing him now."

The phone rings and clicks over. "Mr. Hall's line," I hear his consigliere answer.

"15 calling for Mr. Hall," Agent says.

"One moment."

The phone is muted for no longer than a moment before Ruben answers. "Yes."

"Ruben," I say.

"15, how can I help you?"

"I'm sitting in a room with two soldiers of yours."

He groans. "What have they done?"

"They told me they were going to shove their gun in my mouth while they raped me."

"Who are you?" one of the guys asks.

"You and I have a good working relationship, Ruben. Either I take them out, or I send them back to you and you do it?"

"I'll take care of them, 15. I apologize for any inconvenience they may have caused you. Who are they?"

I look at the two guys. "Names?" Neither say anything, but I patiently wait. "One's about six-one, light brown hair with a scar under his left eye."

"Six-one, light brown hair with a scar under his eye," Ruben repeats as if he's relaying the information. There's a pause from Ruben. "Anthony Pick?"

"Anthony Pick," I say and carefully watch their reaction. My confirmation comes in the way of his eyes widening and his shoulders stiffening. "That's him." Suddenly, this Anthony guy's phone rings. "Answer it," I say.

He slowly reaches into his suit breast pocket and takes his phone out. "Boss?" he answers.

"Both of you get back here, now." I hear this faintly through Ruben's side of our telephone conversation.

"Yes, boss."

Ruben hangs up from them and returns to me. "I'll handle this."

"I look forward to our future business together," I say.

"He's gone," Agent says.

"Who the fuck are you?" Anthony asks.

I feel the chill of satisfaction pebble my skin. With my guns still pointed to them, I smile and say, "15." Both of them instantly groan as the look down at the ground. They know the shit they're in. "Leave. Right now." Wordlessly, they exit the room and head back to Ruben. They didn't even pack.

"Why is it wherever you go, you end up killing someone?"

"I didn't kill them," I point out to Agent.

"You didn't, but you know Ruben will."

"Ruben doesn't get his hands dirty."

"You know what I mean," Agent says.

"They brought this on themselves. It's on them, not me," I pause as I stand and make quick work of retrieving their guns. "Where are they?"

"They're down in the parking garage. I've got eyes on them."

"Make sure they don't come back."

"You know I have eyes everywhere."

I look around the room to make sure I haven't dropped anything, which I know I haven't, and head back to my room. I disconnect my earpiece and take myself into the bathroom. The generous bath is calling me name. As I run the water, I strip off and climb into the bathtub. Leaning my head back, I close my eyes and take several deep breaths as my moments with Ben force themselves to the front of my mind.

I open my eyes and stare up at the ceiling, trying to think why someone would want Ben dead.

I search deep within myself because I know by the time I'm done in Bankstown Creek, Ben Pearson will be dead. I've been paid to kill him; that's what I'm going to do.

I just have to get into Bankstown Creek undetected, go in, and kill him. I'll make it fast by putting a bullet between his eyes. I won't drag it out and torture him. I'll do the job and leave.

It's the only thing I can do.

I'll do it so fast that he won't even know it's coming.

I let out a long drawn out sigh and blink several times. This is the only way.

CHAPTER FOUR

—·—

My alarm startles me out of a restless sleep. I lie under the covers looking out the window, feeling sick to my stomach. This is the last stretch to Bankstown Creek and I'm struggling with what I have to do when I arrive.

I tossed and turned all night, unable to catch more than a few moments' sleep here and there. My mind was racing as I tried to see a clear reason why someone would want Ben dead. There's a heavy lump sitting in the pit of my stomach from the fact Ben lives on the street where I used to live before I was taken. There are so many coincidences in this situation, making it difficult to wrap my head around it.

I look at my phone and roll my eyes at the time. I'm tired and conflicted about what I need to do. I've never killed someone I've had sex with before. It's really playing havoc with my mind. I snicker as I push the covers back and sit on the edge of the bed. "You killed Lucas," I remind myself. "But he doesn't really count," I say to myself as I walk into the bathroom for my morning routine. "He and I both knew that was coming."

Well, maybe he *didn't.*

I finish changing for the day and wheel my suitcase out of the room. I head down to reception where Crystal is again at the front desk. She looks up to see me and immediately averts her eyes. "Good morning," she says with a croak to her voice. "Checking out?"

"Yes, I am." I place the key on the counter and slide it over to her.

"About yesterday." She's still refusing to look at me. "Thank you." She lifts her chin for me to notice her eyes are red and puffy.

"My advice to you is this; do better because no one is going to save you if you're not willing to save yourself."

She finishes doing her checkout procedure and places the receipt on the counter for me. "I will," she finally says. "I'll do much better." Crystal fidgets nervously as she waits for me to leave.

She thinks she knows the danger she might have been in, but in all seriousness, she has no idea at all.

I head down to the garage and to my car, where I start the last part of my journey toward Bankstown Creek. I have to do something to distract myself from how tired I am and from all thoughts of the job ahead of me.

I blare my music as I drive along. Hours of music pumping hard through the stereo system. The music soothes my mind by distracting me from the task ahead. The fact I'm returning home after so many years is also stirring up a buttload of emotions that I've pushed into the pit of hell.

Before I even realize it, I'm nearing Bankstown Creek. I swallow the nervousness back and slide my armor on. I can't let something like personal thoughts or emotions distract me from what I'm here to do.

I glance in my rearview mirror when I see the flash of the red and blue lights. A part of me perks up with excitement at the thought of seeing Ben again. I shake my head attempting to dislodge those dangerous thoughts. No. I'll break into his house and do it while he's sleeping so he doesn't feel a thing. I can't be cruel to him. He hasn't done anything to me to deserve my savagery.

I pull over onto the shoulder and wait for the police officer to approach me. I just don't want it to be Ben. I don't want to see him like this. I have to stay hidden—invisible. I'll watch him from afar, figure out why someone is willing to pay me three million dollars to kill him; then I'll put him down like a wounded animal. *Fast with no pain.*

There's a rapping at the window and my stomach tightens. I look over to see a police officer angled away from me. Lowering my window, I look up at him. "Do you know why I pulled you over?" he asks in a no-nonsense voice.

"No."

"Your music was too loud. I could hear you from two cars back. I had my lights on for a good minute before you saw me and pulled over. That's dangerous for you and for the other drivers on the road." He attempts to intimidate me by standing to his full height with his shoulders pulled back and his chest protruding out.

"Oh," I say in a monotonous drawl.

"Am I boring you?" he asks, his voice stern. "License and registration." He holds his hand out to me and waits.

I look at his badge and it reads AC Ethan Martelli. *Assistant Chief.* Which means he works with Ben.

I play it safe from here on. I reach across to the glove compartment and take out the registration and my alias driver's license. "I'm sorry, Officer Martelli, I've been having a terrible day." I'm hoping he doesn't check over my car because he may find the weapons I have hidden in the trunk. If he finds the weapons I have with me, it'll make for an interesting situation. *For him.*

He takes the papers from me and looks them over. "Mrs. Moore," he starts.

"Miss," I correct him with a smile. Anna Moore isn't my real name, but it's the alias that's cleanest. Anna Moore is a high-profile headhunter. This version of me seeks executives for companies. It's a complete front, but it's functional and serves a purpose. Like when I'm pulled over by police.

"Miss Moore, you're far from home. What are you doing here in Bankstown Creek?"

My armor drops into place; my mask is firmly attached. "I've passed through here a few times, and it's such pretty country that I'm considering buying a cabin here to escape the rat race when things become too much." I flutter my lashes and scan his body as I casually flirt with him.

"Well..." He clears his throat and pulls his shoulders back a little more. Men are such easy creatures to read. A rapid eye blink, maybe a little nibble on my lower lip, and they're like putty in my hands. The Anna charm is turned up to maximum. "I hope you do purchase property here. It's a great place to live." He smiles, hands me my license and registration and taps the top of my car. "Keep the volume down from now on, Miss Moore."

"Of course."

He hesitates for a moment as if he wants to say something to me. Good Lord, he better not dare to ask me out. "I hope to see you again soon, Anna Moore." My skin crawls as he says my name.

"Perhaps you will."

I wait until he walks away, then safely merge back onto the road. Ethan Martelli follows me for a little over two miles and keeps going when I pull into a gas station. There's something about him that I'm not particularly fond of. I'm not sure what it is yet, but if it's anything dangerous, I'll find out. *I always do.*

It takes me another half hour to reach my cabin. Agent procured this cabin for me many years ago, as he has done with all my other safe houses. It's secluded and completely off the grid. As with all my safe houses, the cabin is essentially a reinforced steel box. Nothing can get in without Agent being made aware of it. My phone rings as I pull up in front of the cabin. "Yeah," I answer as I get out.

"Welcome home, boss." I walk around to the trunk of the car and take out my suitcase. "The keypad at the front door is programmed to accept your and my fingerprints."

"*Your* fingerprints? Do you presume you're going to visit me any time soon?" I snicker and roll my eyes.

"Just in case I need to come out there for anything."

I stop rolling my suitcase and tilt my head to the side, knowing Agent has eyes on me. "What, you think you're going to save me if someone tries to attack?"

"Hey, I might be good with a gun," he counters in a hurt, though serious tone.

"When was the last time you shot anything, Agent?"

There's a long pause while he deeply inhales. "That's beside the point."

I chuckle and continue to make my way to the front door. I hold my thumb up to the black pad and it scans my print. The door clicks three times before I can open it. I look around and nod slowly. "Nice."

"Minimalistic, just the way you like it. The fridge and freezer are fully stocked, your weapons room is identical to those in all your other properties. The only thing missing is your customized and personalized Glocks."

I drop my keys on the kitchen counter and walk around the kitchen and dining room. "You did a good job with this one."

"I'm glad you like it." I can hear him smiling with pride. "If you head toward your right, down the back..." I start walking where he says. "Yeah, on the left there's a door leading to your weapons room."

I open the door and smile when I see everything is laid out exactly the way I like it. It makes it easy to gather my weapons quickly. "Looks acceptable," I reply to Agent.

"Acceptable? Here I was waiting for praise and appreciation."

"I said it was acceptable. What more do you want?"

"Maybe something along the lines of, 'Oh, Agent, you're the best assistant I've ever known. I'd never be able to do this without you.' Something like that."

"I see, so you want me to lie." I look up at the camera and smile.

"If only you could see me giving you the one-finger salute." I lift my brows as I wipe the smile off my face. "Okay, okay, I'm kidding, 15."

I lower my phone and end the call. I walk out of the weapons room and roll my suitcase over to inspect the rest of the cabin. I find two fairly large bedrooms, both with en suite bathrooms and walk-in closets. I take the room facing the front and unpack before I call Agent back. "Is the security system connected to my phone?"

"You hung up on me so abruptly that I thought I'd hurt your feelings." I look up toward the camera in the bedroom and stare at it. "Man, your sense of humor has gone out the window. Speaking of windows, just like all your other properties—bulletproof glass."

"Is it connected, or not?" I repeat, already bored with Agent's constant need for reassurance.

"I'm connecting it now."

I hang up and sit on the edge of the bed. I bring the cameras up on my phone and see where everything is positioned. I take the next half hour walking the perimeter to see if there are any blind spots someone could exploit for a surprise attack. I tap my earpiece to connect with Agent again. "I've identified two problems and need them remedied."

"Where?" I walk into a spot and stand still exactly where the two cameras don't meet. "Left arm out to the side." I lift my left arm. "And now your right." I lower my left and lift my right. "Take a step forward." I do. "Another." I take another step. "Take three steps back." I do that too. "I've got the coordinates for that spot. Where's the next?"

"It's on the other side of the cabin."

"Is that near the shed by the bottom left?"

"Yeah, it is."

"I knew about that one, but wanted to wait for you in case you found another spot. But I'll get you to head down there so I can see exactly what needs to be done."

I walk to the shed and stand in the blind spot. "Here."

"Move your left arm straight out." I do. "Yeah, I've got that too. I'll get on those."

"I'm heading into town to do some recon. Get it fixed by the time I return."

"Already on it."

I tap my earpiece off and make my way back into the cabin. I retrieve my car keys from the kitchen counter and head into town to start my research on Ben Pearson.

Bankstown Creek isn't a large town, not in comparison to a city. But it's still large enough that I'm able to move around without the townsfolk taking notice of me. It's a passing-through community, so it works well for me. I'll be able to slip in, do my research, do my job, and slide right out without being detected.

I drive past the police station first and glance inside. Next, I want to head over to Lionsgate Road so I can break into Ben's house to try and figure out why there's a hit on him. As I'm driving through town toward Lionsgate Road, I glance at a small supermarket. My eye catches a police cruiser, and

I make a hard right into the parking lot. "What am I doing?" I ask myself as I sit in the car for a moment once I'm parked.

If that's Ben, then I should remain invisible because I don't want him to know I'm here. That would make killing him more complicated than it already is. I look down at the steering wheel as I attempt to talk myself out of doing one of the most reckless things I've ever done.

"This isn't me," I say as I shake my head and attempt to pull myself together. I take several deep breaths, attempting to calm my racing mind. I need to regain my composure and deal with whatever is going on in my head.

Without listening to a single shred of reason, I turn my car off, grab my phone and get out of the car. *What is wrong with me?* I scan the area, careful about who sees me as I make my way into the supermarket. "Hi," one of the employees greets me.

I give her a nod, then head straight down to the dairy section to grab a carton of milk as my cover.

My heart leaps into my throat when I see Ben standing in front of the bread, speaking to someone on the phone. God damn, he's so much more attractive than I remember him to be. His suit is snug and perfectly fitted as I survey his body.

He reaches for a loaf of bread but stops himself as his conversation becomes more heated. I move so I can discreetly listen in on what he's saying. I'm gifted with the cover of a woman attempting to quiet her crying baby while pushing her cart.

"Listen," his voice rises tightly but he stops when the woman with the baby darts her hand out for a loaf of bread. "We'll discuss this later."

Discuss what? And with whom? The woman continues down the aisle and I keep listening to him.

"Now's not the time." Maybe there's more to Ben than I thought. Shit, he's not married, is he? I don't screw married men. I'll fucking kill him for that reason alone.

Something inside me clicks and I know I won't be able to do my reconnaissance without him seeing me. I walk up to stand beside him as I search for a loaf of bread. He glances over at me, then does a double take. "I have to go." He hangs up and slides his phone into his suit pocket. "Anna Moore," he says in his sexy, velvety voice.

I mimic his double take as my mouth opens in surprise. "Ben Pearson." I smile as I return my attention to the bread.

"What are you doing here in Bankstown Creek? I honestly thought I'd never see you again."

That was the plan, but plans change. "I'm out this way because I'm looking for a cabin to buy."

His brows rise as he flicks a look down my body. "You don't strike me as the cabin type of girl."

I step back and softly laugh. "Why, what type of girl do you take me for?"

"One who likes the expensive things in life. A beautiful bubble bath while sipping on champagne and eating chocolate-dipped strawberries."

I hold my free hand up and shake my head. "You've got me. You already know the type of woman I am." Ben's smile reaches his eyes. He looks genuinely happy to see me, which saddens me because I'm here to do a hit. *On him.*

"Considering you left so abruptly when we first met, I think you should allow me to take you out to dinner." This might be the opportunity I need to get close to Ben Pearson, find out why a hit was ordered on him, kill him, and collect the rest of my money. There has to be a reason someone wants him dead.

"You know, Ben..." I nibble on my lower lip, bringing his attention to my mouth. "I'm rather..." I drag my eyes down over his taut body and smile. "Ravenous."

Ben visibly gulps at my audacity in openly eye-fucking him. He clears his throat and looks up and down the aisle. "Good thing there's a diner across the street. It might not look like much, but the food is good." He steps closer to me and I pull in a ragged breath. I have to stop thinking with my vagina and start thinking with my head. I have to start thinking of him as a hit, and not a person with a name. "Let me finish up and I'll meet you outside in about ten minutes." He steps closer and kisses me on the cheek. His mouth lingers longer than a platonic kiss should. I close my eyes and appreciate the woodsy scent of his cologne. His right hand snakes down to find the small of my back as he gently pulls me into him. The moment is broken when he drops his hand and steps back. There's a delicious fire burning in his eyes and a small smile tugs at his lips. "I won't be long."

I pull myself together and push down the electricity crackling through my body. I arch a brow and lift a shoulder. "You'd better not be long, or I might just leave."

I take several steps backward and watch Ben chuckle as he runs his hand through his hair. I walk to the front and pay for the milk I bought, then head out to sit in my car. I wrestle with what I'm going to do. I need to focus, do some recon work, and get this hit done. I can't let my feelings get in the way of a job. I've been paid to provide a service, and I need to follow through and perform the task I've been contracted for.

Lowering my chin, I shake my head as I think about the task at hand. Ben Pearson is a target. He's a hit worth three million dollars. I can't let this become personal. Glancing up, I'm rewarded with the sight of Ben leaving the grocery store. Even his walk drips with sex appeal. His head is high, his shoulders pulled back and his chest is strong. *Damn.*

He looks around for me, and when he notices me standing by my car he makes a beeline for me. "Do you want to follow me? The diner is quite literally across the road and down a block. Or we could walk."

There are weapons in my trunk. I'm not leaving my car unattended. "I'll follow you."

He taps the hood of my car as he walks back to his police cruiser. I can't tear my eyes off of him. There's something about a man in a suit that makes my heart flutter. Or maybe it's just this one particular man that causes palpitations. I really have to stop thinking with my vagina.

He backs out of the spot he was in and pulls in front of me. He juts his head to the side, indicating I should follow him. My mind is racing with every dirty thing I want us to do together as I drive behind him the two minutes down the road.

I pull into a space beside Ben. I don't even have a chance to reach for my phone in the center console before he opens the driver's door. "I was hoping you were going to have second thoughts and take off, which means I would've had to chase you and maybe even throw the cuffs on you for attempting to evade the police."

I slide out of the car and purposely stand a hair's breadth away from him. I look down at his lips, then back up to his eyes. "You'd have to catch me first, and there's no way in the world you'd be able to." I step back and let him close the door.

Ben's eyes widen as he shakes his head and smiles. "I'm in trouble when it comes to you, aren't I?" he innocently asks.

Way more than you could ever imagine. "Maybe."

"This is the place I was talking about." He steps aside and opens the door for me. "Ma'am." Ben gestures inside.

"Look at that, a real-life gentleman."

He darts his hand out and grabs my upper arm, stopping me from entering the diner. He pulls me close into his chest and leans down to whisper, "Not between the sheets."

My skin tingles with desire and my heartbeat quickens with the promise of what's to come. I shake my head slightly as I attempt to dislodge the excitement burning through me. "You can hope you'll have me again," I say with sass as I walk into the diner. "And you know what they say about living in hope."

"Hello." The waitress flicks her gaze at who's coming in behind me and her eyes light up. "Hey there, Ben," she says.

"Hi, Tammy. Can we grab a table please?"

"Sure thing." She takes two menus and peers around the diner. "Booth or table?"

"Booth," I say before Ben has a chance to answer. I need to be able to keep an eye on everyone coming and going.

"Sure thing, follow me this way." Tammy turns and smiles at me. "Hello. I haven't seen you around."

"I'm passing through," I reply as I carefully check my surroundings.

"Here you go." She places the menus on the table and steps back. "I'm also your waitress tonight, so I'll be back in a few minutes." She flashes a smile toward us, and this gives me the opportunity to really look at her. Tammy is, for the lack of a better word, plastic. Her boobs sit unusually high, her forehead doesn't move, and her capped teeth are nearly obscenely white. But she seems docile enough.

"Thank you, Tammy," Ben says. She leaves, and Ben slides a menu over to me before taking the other and casually perusing it. "I think you missed me," he says without even lifting his chin to look at me. *Trust me, I don't miss.* "And you remembered where I live and work so you decided to find me."

If only he knew the real reason I'm here. "Sure, let's go with that," I say with a smile.

He chuckles as he keeps looking over the menu. He takes another moment, then lifts his head. "Do you know what you want to eat yet?"

Yep, you. I close my eyes for a moment to regain my composure. "Clearly you come here a lot, or Tammy wouldn't know you by name."

"Everyone knows me here. After all, I am the police chief." He glances over at Tammy and nods. "But yes, I do come here often."

"What do you recommend?"

"The burger is good. The loaded fries are too. The wild rice soup is the best in the state, and the booyah is probably some of the best I've ever had."

I haven't had wild rice soup since before Damon and Nox. I push those emotions down too. I'm here for work, not to reminisce about the past. "A burger it is."

Right on cue Tammy shows up. "You ready to order?" She flips her little book open and brings her pen up to it, ready for us.

"Two burgers and fries please, Tammy," Ben says. "And I'll have a soda." He looks to me.

"I'll have a soda too, please."

"Sure thing," Tammy says as she writes our order down before backing away and leaving.

"So, what brings you into my small community?"

This is where my façade really needs to be convincing. Lucky for me, I'm good at remaining calm and lying. "Looking to buy a vacation property around here. A small cottage or cabin where I can escape when I need some peace."

"Why Bankstown Creek?" Ben's lips purse together as he cocks a brow. Clearly he has a healthy dose of doubt.

"Why *not* Bankstown Creek? Are you trying to tell me you don't want me here?"

"God, no!" he backpedals quickly. "If anything, I'd like to see a lot more of you here."

"Is that so?"

Out of the corner of my eye, I see Ethan Martelli pull into the parking lot. He parks beside my car and gets out of his police cruiser. He glances into my car, then looks into the diner. "Tell me about you, Anna."

While keeping an eye on Ethan, I take in a deep breath and give a slight shrug. "Not much to tell."

"Do you have any siblings?"

"I don't. I'm an only child."

"What about your parents?"

"What about my parents?"

"Where do they live? What do they do?"

I clear my throat, feeling uneasy at answering questions about them. I hesitate for a few seconds and straighten my shoulders when Ethan walks into the diner and heads straight over to where Ben and I are sitting. I glance over Ben's shoulder, making him turn to see what I'm looking at. "Miss Moore, I see you've already met our chief of police." He shoves his hands in his pockets as he stands beside our booth.

"Ethan, what are you doing here?" Ben asks.

"Stopped by for a bite to eat and I saw Anna's car. Thought I'd come in and say hello."

"How do you know Anna?" Ben looks between us, confused.

"I was playing my music too loud on the way into town and Ethan pulled me over."

"Did he cite you?"

"He was kind enough to let me off with a warning."

"I'm so rude, I should properly introduce myself." Ethan takes his hand out of his pocket and extends it to me. "Ethan Martelli."

I reach for his hand and take it in mine. The moment my fingers wrap around his hand my skin crawls and the hair on the back of my neck stands on end. There's something wrong with him. My stomach churns and I'm hyperaware this man is hiding something.

"You already know my name." I plaster on a saccharine smile as I slowly pull my hand away from him.

"How's the hunt for a cabin going?" Ethan asks as he folds his hands in front of his chest.

Pain radiates through my hands as I ball them into fists beneath the table. My fingers are itching to reach for a gun, but I can't do anything in such a public place. "Considering I only got in late this afternoon, I haven't had time to start yet."

"Where are you staying?" Ethan asks innocently, though I know he's assessing me.

"An Air BNB," I reply and arch a brow at him. I want him gone. I don't want him near me, not until I can research who the fuck he is.

Ethan holds eye contact with me a moment too long, making Ben clear his throat. "Okay, well, I think I better go pick up my food," Ethan says. "Nice to officially meet you, Anna."

"You too." I look to Ethan and give him a small nod.

"See you at work tomorrow, boss." He claps a hand to Ben's shoulder, and I do everything in my power not to leap over the table and rip his hand off of Ben. I chew on the inside of my cheek as I watch Ethan head toward the door.

"Here are your drinks, and your burgers should be out soon," Plastic Tammy happily announces.

"You were telling me about yourself before we were interrupted." Ben picks his soda up and takes a sip. I can't help but focus on his mouth and wish it was on me.

Damn it, stop thinking of him like that. "Nothing much to say. An only child."

"Kids?"

"What about them?" I ask as I drag the tall glass of soda over toward me.

"Do you have any?"

"Do you?"

He laughs and shakes his head. "No, I don't have any kids." He pointedly looks at me.

"Nor do I."

"Been married before?"

"Why do I feel like you're interrogating me?"

He holds his hands up in surrender. "I'm trying to get to know you, that's all."

Ethan has put me on the defensive, and I need to take it down a notch. "No, I haven't ever been married. What about you?"

"God, no! I'm married to my job." He looks down at his soda and raises his brows.

"You're a player then. Or as the kids these days say, are you a fuck-boy?"

Ben lifts his gaze to focus on me. A small smirk tugs at the corners of his lips. "I'm definitely not a fuck-boy." His brows rise as he laughs once again. "Fuck-boy, what a stupid phrase." He sips his soda once more. "Tell me about your parents."

I feel my body become rigid. This is a topic of conversation I don't like talking about. "Not much to say about them. Mom abandoned Dad and me after I was born, and Dad died when I was fifteen."

"Oh, I'm sorry. Did you fall into the system?"

"No, I didn't. A friend took me in." Lucas was anything *but* a friend. "What about you?"

"I have two sisters, and my parents passed away years ago. Nothing sordid or even interesting."

This is where I need to probe and attempt to get as much information as I can. "No extra-curricular activities?"

"Like what?" he asks as he relaxes back in the booth and watches me.

"Oh, I don't know. Maybe you wear black clothes and fight crime under the cover of night."

He smirks. "Like Batman?"

"Wow." I lift my brows and look away. "You automatically thought of yourself as a superhero."

"Isn't that what you're implying though?" he quickly retorts.

"I was going for Cat Woman, but hey." I wink at Ben. "If you think you're Batman."

"I'll have you know I look damn fine in a catsuit." He wiggles his finger at me playfully. "But no, nothing too over the top outside of work. What about you? What do you do for fun?"

I look outside and think about an acceptable answer to his question. *Target practice. Cleaning my weapons.* "I like to read."

"Don't tell me, I think you're a classics sort of woman."

More like studying my next hit. "I like anything that holds my attention." Especially research on my next target. I glance outside again and notice Ethan Martelli is still across the road, sitting in his car watching us.

Tammy silently places our burgers down in front of us and takes a small step back. "Is there anything else I can get you?"

"I'm good, thank you." I smile up at her, fully aware that Ethan is across the street.

"I'm good too, Tammy." Ben picks his burger up and takes a massive bite. I mimic his actions because I'm quite hungry. "I think after we eat you should come back to my house."

I chew and swallow before playfully saying, "Why's that?"

"So I can rip your clothes off and tongue fuck you," he says casually.

Yes, that would be acceptable, thank you. I clear my filthy thoughts long enough to remember I'm here to kill him, not to fuck him. A part of me is toying with the idea of doing both. First fuck him, then kill him. But that part is quickly overshadowed with the controlled always-in-work-mode part that screams how bad an idea that is. I shouldn't get too involved. Once this job is done, I'll have to live with myself for liking him and killing him.

This isn't personal, Ben Pearson. "What a tempting offer," I finally respond while internally fighting with myself.

"It's settled."

"No, it's not. I've had a long drive and I'm quite tired."

"I have a bed," he cheekily offers.

"Which we wouldn't be sleeping in," I counter.

He flicks his hand dismissively. "Semantics." He grabs a few fries and shoves them into his mouth. "I mean eventually we'd sleep—after a thorough workout."

I can't help but smile. "Like I said, it's a tempting offer. However, my answer remains the same. Not tonight." Besides, I need to get back to the cabin and have Agent look into Ethan Martelli.

"You're missing out on riding my face," he attempts to persuade me.

I nearly choke at his words but manage to keep my control and composure. "Well, if you're putting it that way." He proudly smirks. "It's a still a no."

"I could arrest you, throw the cuffs on you and take you back to my house where I'll have my wicked ways with you."

The cuffs would be off before you even knew what was happening. "Now that we're talking about cuffs and kidnapping, that changes everything," I say with mirth in my voice.

"It does?" Ben's eyes light up.

"No." I take another bite of my burger and watch as Ben's lips droop in disappointment. "I'll make you a deal though."

"What?"

"Maybe I'll let you take me to lunch tomorrow."

Nonchalantly he shrugs. "Maybe I'm busy tomorrow."

"Forget I said anything then," I say as if I don't care.

"Wait! No...no." He points at me. "Lunch tomorrow is good."

"Lunch sounds fantastic, I'm so glad you suggested it."

Ben nudges the rest of his fries around. "I'm going to make a bold statement, Anna."

"Yeah? What's that?" I pick my napkin up and wipe my hands, then push the plate to the side.

"I have a feeling, when it comes to you, I'm in over my head."

"You have no idea," I honestly reply.

Tammy approaches us and reaches for my plate. "All done? Can I take this?"

"Of course, thank you."

She looks at Ben, who crumples his napkin and tosses it on the plate. "I'm done too, Tammy. I'll take the check when you're ready." Tammy stacks my plate on top of Ben's and leaves. "You sure I can't interest you in coming back home with me?"

My vagina is screaming at me to go. "As much as the offer of having your tongue buried inside me is something I'm certainly keen for..." I expel a long sigh. "I'm going to have to take a rain check."

Tammy places the slip of paper face down on the table, and I nimbly reach out to snatch it. "I should be paying," Ben argues as he holds his hand out and wiggles his fingers at me.

"Why?"

"Because it's the right thing to do."

I scoot out of the bench seat and stand. "You should've been quicker then." I take the slip of paper and walk up to the front so I can pay for our burgers.

Ben walks ahead and waits by the door, then opens it once I've paid and I'm heading out. He walks me over to my car and stands close to me. Ben steps in closer, trapping me between him and my driver's door. He leans into me and slowly bends to place a heated kiss on my cheek. "Are you absolutely sure I can't change your mind?"

My heart is thrumming with excitement. I reach forward and wrap his tie around my hand. I pull him in closer and skim my mouth against his. I like how close he is to me but I prefer us to be even closer. My skin tingles with a burning desire for Ben to touch me. His eyes darken and he steps even closer to me. I need to break my irrational behavior. "Good night, Mr. Pearson." I tilt my head up and pepper kisses across his jaw. The feel of his stubble scraping against my lips is delicious torture.

"Anna." He sucks in a breath and steps backward, putting distance between us. He buttons his suit jacket to camouflage the bulge in his pants.

I open the door to my car and slide in. Backing out of the spot, I see Ethan Martelli still in his car, watching us.

I make sure to peel out of the parking lot quick enough that for Ethan to follow me would be obvious.

Now, I need to head back to the cabin to get some sleep before I start my research on Ben Pearson.

And Ethan Martelli.

CHAPTER FIVE

After a restless night, I finally managed to close my eyes sometime after four in the morning. Now, the warmth of the sun beating through the bulletproof glass window gently wakes me from my terrible sleep.

I push the covers back and head into the bathroom to shower before I start my research on Ben and Ethan. Turning the water on I check to make sure it's come to temperature before stepping into it. I extend my hands in front of me to lean on the tiled wall, close my eyes and allow the water to cascade down over my body. Images of Ben haunt me as I stand under the constant stream of hot water.

Killing him will be hard enough without my feelings interfering with the job. I open my eyes and straighten. I can't think of him as a man with a name. He's a job.

I suck in a breath and tighten my resolve. He's a target. Nothing more. *Pull yourself together, Anna.* I finish in the shower and step out. Wrapping towels around my body and hair, I walk into the kitchen to make myself a coffee and breakfast. Thinking of Ben in any other way than a target is dangerous, and I can't afford to lose my reputation in this business.

As the coffee brews, I head back to the bedroom to dress. Once done, I grab my laptop and earpiece before heading back to the kitchen to butter toast and sip on my black coffee. I pop the earpiece in and dial Agent. "Morning, 15."

I open my laptop and it springs to life. "Can you patch me into the human resource files for the police department?"

"I can. Are we researching the target?"

My skin erupts into goose bumps when Agent refers to Ben so coldly. I clear my throat, "Yes, I am." I need to investigate Ethan too, but for now, I'll keep my focus on Ben.

I hear him typing on the keyboard, then a window pops up on my laptop screen. "I've got you in," he says.

I click on his file and read what human resources has on file. "He's never had any disciplinary issues."

"Recorded," Agent says.

"No, look at his record. He did four years in narcotics, then four years as a sergeant on the bomb squad."

"Sounds like a bore."

I smirk and keep reading. "Interesting. It shows even though he excelled on the bomb squad, he wanted to go back to narcotics."

"Family reasons? What family? He doesn't have one."

"Look at the date he requested it, and how quickly it was accepted. Something like this request ordinarily takes months, sometimes even longer to be processed." I keep clicking and reading his file. "Another two years in narcotics before he was promoted again."

"He moves fast," Agent verbalizes what I'm thinking.

I hang up on Agent as I continue reading. Ben's spent a total of nearly twelve years in the force and he's rapidly moved up. According to his personnel file, he has no children, wife, ex-wife, or any type of partner. I have to be honest, it's impressive how diligent and hardworking he's been.

It's easy to see how he's climbed the ranks to become chief of police in Bankstown Creek.

I open another window and within seconds, Agent has me hacked into Ben's bank account without having to call him to do the work. Ben has a reasonable mortgage and a small savings account. His pay is deposited into his account and he moves money over to his savings and his mortgage. There are no red flags or anything that appears unreasonable with his account. Public servant pay is quite dismal at best, especially considering his position in the force. My phone rings and I tap the earpiece to answer. "What is it?"

"I've found something."

I open another screen and wait. "What?"

"Have a look at what I'm putting up on your screen."

I wait as it loads on my laptop. "Well," I say as I tap my fingers beside the laptop. "What have we got here?" There's an offshore account in Ben's name with several million dollars in it.

"Every month there's a deposit of fifty thousand, going back for some time."

"Yeah, I see. But, there are no withdrawals. Can you find who's making the deposits?"

"You're not going to believe this, 15, but I can't find the originating accounts the deposits are coming from."

"What? How is that possible?"

"I have no idea, but whoever's putting money in the account is covering their tracks extremely well."

"And you can't find them?"

"I'll keep digging around, but we're not dealing with an average hacker, 15."

"Keep me updated." I take the earpiece out and toss it beside my laptop. Why would someone be putting money into his account? And why are there are no withdrawals? I sit back on the sofa as I stare at the screen. Something isn't right with this account. I chew on the inside of my cheek as I try to imagine some reason as to why he has millions he's not touching. I stare at my half-eaten toast and now-empty coffee cup thinking about what all of this means. Perhaps Ben isn't just a police officer. Maybe there's a legitimate reason for someone wanting him dead. Being in law enforcement means he could arrange things around him to his benefactor's satisfaction quite easily and not get caught. He can move anything around. Weapons, drugs, evidence, even people. If I find out he's into human trafficking, I'll take him down with my bare hands and I'll make sure he suffers.

Noticing the time, I close my laptop and push off the sofa to get ready for my lunch date with Ben. I have to keep him at arm's length while I work out who he is and what he's into. For now I need to get ready.

Ben would find it suspicious if I called him to ask about our lunch date considering we haven't exchanged numbers yet. I already have his number from my research. So, instead of calling him, I'll show up at the station and surprise him. He's probably trying to figure out how to get in contact with me.

I'm heading for the station when I see the familiar flash of red and blue lights behind me, roughly ten miles outside town.

I pull over and watch in my rearview mirror as the familiar, menacing Ethan Martelli exits the police car. He glances around to make sure no other drivers stop or take notice of him. His actions are so obvious. He's pulled me over out on a relatively quiet road that doesn't have a lot of through traffic.

He walks up to the car and I lower my window. "Good to see you, Anna," he starts with a dangerously fake tone.

"Officer Martelli." I smile up at him. "Do you need to see my license again?"

He looks around once more and leans one hand on the top of my car as he angles his body into my space. "I insist you call me Ethan." He smiles and casts a sleazy eye over my chest, slowly lifting his leer back to my eyes. "I was heading back to the station and recognized your car. I thought I'd see how you're liking Bankstown Creek so far. Maybe there's something I can do to make your stay here more comfortable. Where exactly did you say you're staying?"

He's fishing for information, trying to find out as much about me as he can. I must give him the same vibes he gives me. I know he's hiding something, and I think he knows I'm hiding something too. "A friend's house," I reply without giving him shit.

"Which is where?" He draws his brows in together and tilts his head to the side in question.

"Do you need something? I'm on my way to the station and I'm already running late for my lunch with Ben."

"Are you two together?"

"I think that's a whole lot of none-of-your-business." I stare at him for a moment before smiling. "Can I go?"

"I mean if you're not together, perhaps I can take you out for dinner?"

This has nothing to do with attraction. All this is, is him wanting to know who I am and if I'm a threat to him. Hell yeah, buddy, I'm a fucking threat alright. "Dinner?" I nearly laugh out loud. "With you?"

He straightens and looks around once again. "I want to know who's in my town, Anna. I'm protective of what's mine, and we both know, you're..." His jaw relaxes and he clears his throat. I wait another second for him to finish what he was going to say, but he shakes his head and says nothing instead. Wow, I've successfully managed to get under his skin in such a short period of time.

"It must be difficult for you to see a new face in town. Maybe it's best if we do get together for dinner." This will be my best option for gathering as much information about him as I can. "Besides, I completely know what you mean when you say you're protective of what's yours." I cock a brow and smile sweetly.

Touch Ben and I'll kill you.

Ethan nods ever so slightly. He takes a card out of his back pocket and hands it to me. "I'll be expecting your call so we can make arrangements for dinner." I'm surprised he didn't insist on my number. "Until we meet again," he says with a menacing voice.

I pop my clutch and the car takes off sideways off the shoulder and into the driving lane. I glance at the card in the center console as I head toward the police station. I have to find out what Ethan wants. Or better yet, what he's hiding here in Bankstown Creek. Something isn't right with him, and I'm going to discover what his secret is. When I do, God have mercy on his soul.

The police station is like a moment frozen in time. Not one thing has changed in the thirteen years of my absence. My throat constricts as I walk into the station. I have so many memories of when Dad was the police chief of Bankstown Creek. My heart quickens as I almost anticipate him walking out from his office to greet me.

"Hello, can I help you?" My memory is disrupted by a female clerk standing behind the counter.

I swallow twice to dislodge the lump in my throat and smile at her. "I'm here to see Ben Pearson."

"I'll see if he's here. What's your name?" She slides a piece of paper in front of her and lifts a pen.

"Just let him know Anna's here."

"Anna?" She waits for my last name.

"He'll know who I am."

She lifts a brow and nods. "Sure, give me a moment." She disappears through the door that leads to the back of the station.

This place really hasn't changed at all. Not a single thing. Not even the paint color. Even the desks behind the counter are in exactly the same positions as what they used to be. The woman has disappeared toward the rooms in the back and to the right, which was where Dad's office used to be. It's likely Ben's office now. She returns and talks to one of the deputies who shakes her head and lifts her shoulders. The clerk glances toward me, smiles, then picks up the phone and starts talking with someone.

She hangs up within a few moments and looks up wearing a sweet smile. "Ben's out but said he'll be here within the next ten minutes or so."

"Thank you." I slowly pace back and forth but keep an eagle eye on the cars passing by. It's not long before I see Ben's car pull up beside mine. He jogs up to the front door, yanks the door open, and throws his arms around me. This very public display of affection has somewhat unsettled me. I pat his back awkwardly as I glance at the clerk. She smiles and quickly averts her gaze to look at her computer screen. "Ben," I manage to croak as he tightens his embrace.

"I'm glad you came," he whispers and places a tender kiss on my cheek before stepping back. "I'm off today. How do you feel about me cooking for you?" He pulls his shoulders back proudly.

My stomach churns with unease knowing I still have a task to complete, but my skin tingles with excitement at the thought of him cooking for me. "You can cook?"

"Can I ever." He smiles as he links our hands together. He turns to the clerk and gives her a small nod.

"Good, because I'm hungry."

"Follow me back to my house and I'll cook you a feast."

"A feast?" I ask and smirk. "Wow, so you're a gourmet chef," I tease as we walk toward our cars.

We stop when we reach the front of my car. "Actually, I like watching you eat." The tips of his ears turn pink. "And I really want to get to know more about you. So, what better way than to have you come to my house? We won't be interrupted by anyone, and I can cook for you."

This'll give me the perfect opportunity to access his house and do my own investigation. And I want to see where on the street he lives in relation

to where my old house was before Damon and Nox. "Not being interrupted, hmmm, now that sounds like fun."

He leans down and places a small kiss on my lips. "Follow me." He opens
the door to my car and waits until I'm in before he closes it.

I pull out of the spot and wait for him to maneuver his car in front of
mine. I know Ben lives on the street where I grew up. I'm silently praying
his house is on the other end from where my home was before Damon and
Nox killed my father and blew it up.

My heart beats faster as we approach Lionsgate Road. My palms sweat
and I can't help but clench my jaw. He rounds the corner onto Lionsgate
and my stomach twists as he slows his car and pulls into a driveway.

Shit, this is *exactly* where my home used to be.

I park behind his car and look up and down the street. So much has
changed in the thirteen years I've been absent. When I lived here there
were only, I think, three houses on the street including ours. Now, it's been
broken up into smaller lots and there are at least ten newer houses. I sit
in my car for a moment attempting to calm my response to being back
here after so many years. Ben exits his car and waits for me to meet him. A
massive part of me doesn't want to be here, but I have a job to do.

He stares at me as I slowly walk toward him. "Everything okay? You look
pale."

"Do I?" I have to switch into cold-hearted assassin, not the sentimental
fool I fear I've become. "This is a pretty street." I look at the trees lining the
wide road.

"Yeah, I like how quiet it is, which is why I bought this house." I feel sick
as we head toward his front door. I find myself wringing the hem of my
t-shirt with numb hands while my stomach quivers uneasily. Ben unlocks
the door and steps aside, allowing me to go in first. "Hey, are you sure

you're okay? If you're uncomfortable here we can always head back into town for lunch."

He's misread my trepidation for fear of being alone with him. "I'm not uncomfortable at all, I've..." I tap my head. "There's a lot going on at the moment."

"Anything I can help you with?"

You have no idea. "No, there's nothing you can do to help. Thank you, though."

He walks slightly ahead of me and leads me into his kitchen. "I know this is going to seem presumptuous of me, but I made a lasagna last night for lunch today."

I can't help the belly laugh that escapes me. "That's so cute! I've never had a man make me lasagna before."

"So you're okay with it?" He opens the fridge and takes out a deep glass dish. Ben lifts the aluminum foil from the top and proudly shows me his handiwork. "I made this," he says as he eagerly looks to me for his approval.

This has to be the most generous thing anyone has ever done for me. "It looks delicious."

He turns the oven on and slides the lasagna into it. "I need to reheat it, but it won't take long. I hope you're hungry." I walk further into the kitchen, lean against the counter, and stare at him. "What?" Once the food is in the oven, he returns to the fridge and takes out a pepper, tomatoes, a cucumber and lettuce. "What?" he repeats as he places them on the counter and turns toward me.

Silently, I push off the counter and step toward him. Fisting the collar of his t-shirt in my fingers, I drag him down toward me and ferociously attack his mouth. Ben uses his body to push me up against the counter where he snakes his hands down to grip my ass, *hard*. The delicious bite of his strong fingers causes a small moan to bubble through me.

"Fuck," he growls against my lips.

I can feel his hard cock straining against his jeans, and all I want is to tear his clothes off and fuck him right here in the kitchen. I bite on his lower lip, nearly breaking the skin. He tastes as good as I remember him. I want him. I want to do dirty imaginative things to him. I also want him to do those things to me. My throat constricts with the knowledge that I'm going to have to put him down like a wounded animal in the coming days, and I just stop. It's not right that I do this to him, or to me. I push Ben away while I step away from him. "Bathroom?"

Ben's face holds so many questions when he points down the hallway. I don't wait for further instructions from him; I leave and head to the bathroom. Closing the door behind me, I make sure it's locked before I run the water from the faucet to give me enough time to gather my thoughts.

I look in the mirror and stare at myself as I take several deep breaths. Dad taught me that when it's challenging, I have to regain my control, and the best way to start is with my breath. If I can control my breathing, I can control my emotions, and if I can control my emotions, I can control myself and my reaction to the situation I'm in.

I need to make sure I don't let anything cloud my focus on the reason I'm here. I can't let something as simple as a damn lasagna distract me from my job.

Okay, I'm ready to place my attention on what I need to do. *Kill Ben.*

I turn the faucet off, and pull my shoulders back. Opening the door, I walk back out to the kitchen. "Are you okay?" Ben asks as he slices the cucumber and places the slices on top of the salad.

I could easily overpower him and take the knife from him. I could slice his throat open and kill him right now. "I'm fine." I eye the knife but decide to make this painless for him.

"Well, lunch should be ready soon. There are a few minutes left on the timer for the lasagna and the salad only needs dressing now."

"Where did you learn to cook?" I ask as I prop myself up on a stool on the opposite side of the counter.

A smile slowly stretches his lips. "I loved cooking starting from back in college. It's something I've loved since I made my first pancake. I started experimenting, and now I love to cook. My sisters make fun of me, but that's okay. It's only because I'm better at it than they are." He leans his elbows on the counter and reaches for my hands, but I pull them back. "What is it?"

I have to strengthen my armor so he can't see my agitation. "I think it's best if we take this slow."

"Slow?" Ben's forehead crinkles. He straightens and his jaw becomes tight and rigid. "Slow?" he repeats as he runs his hand through his hair. "When you left my hotel room, I never thought I'd see you again. And then, by chance, you happen to be in my town and you want to take things slow?"

It's not by chance. "It's for the best, Ben," I say, trying not to give anything away.

"Best for you or for me?"

"Both," I counter immediately. "I'm here only until I find a vacation home, then I leave and return home."

He averts his eyes and looks down at the salad. "Tell me a bit about you."

"Nothing interesting to tell. I'm an only child, and my father died, but you already know all of that."

"What was your dad like?"

I wasn't expecting him to ask. My heart jolts as I recall my dad. "He was..." I push off the stool and walk away from Ben. "He was amazing. He taught me how to be the person I am."

"It seems like he did a wonderful job with you."

"He did everything he could for me, and I wouldn't be where I am today if it wasn't for him. I'm grateful for the time we had together, even though it was only fifteen years." I cross my arms in front of my chest and push those feelings down as far as I can.

"Do you miss him?"

"Every damned day," I answer too honestly. Jesus, what am I doing? Why am I letting my mask slip?

"What did your dad do?" My back straightens as ice scrapes over my spine. Thankfully the timer on the oven goes off and I'm given a reprieve. I don't have to answer Ben's question. "The lasagna is ready." Ben puts on oven mitts and lifts the glass dish out.

"Smells good."

He places the dish on a trivet on the kitchen counter. Grabbing two plates and two sets of flatware, he sets the counter for us. "Sit." He looks pointedly at the stool.

I walk back to where I was sitting and wait until he's ready before I sit. Ben rounds the counter with a spatula and sits beside me. "You were telling me about what your dad did before he passed away."

"He was a cop too."

"Was he? Where?"

I pick a small town I know Ben hasn't worked before. "Fort Yallina," I say, knowing he has no idea where that is.

"Where is that?"

"California," I lie effortlessly.

"Never heard of it." He shrugs, then cuts the lasagna into quarters. "Hope you're hungry."

"Starving."

"So, you said a friend took you in when your dad passed away. How did you cope with that?"

"What do you mean?" I cut into my food and eat some. "This is good."

"I told you I could cook." He smiles cheekily. "I mean, you seem so well-adjusted, considering your mom abandoned you and your dad passed away when you were young."

My fork stops in midair as I turn to stare at Ben. "Well-adjusted? What does that even mean?"

"Clearly you have your wits about you."

"I guess so. I'm not a serial killer." I snicker at my words. I've woven an intricate web of lies for everyone not in my inner circle. From the outside, I appear like an ordinary twenty-eight-year old woman whose career is at its pinnacle. I look good on paper. In real life, if someone researches me, they'll find a career-driven woman who has no ties to anyone.

"It's comforting to know I don't have a serial killer in my home, although, isn't that just what a serial killer would say in order to get people to believe that they're normal?"

"Normal?" I roll my eyes and smirk. "There's no such thing as normal anymore."

He leans over and rubs my shoulder with his. "I like you, Anna, and I think you like me too."

If only the problem was me liking him. "You're alright," I say with a small smile, trying to deflect from what I fear is about to come.

"I'm taking that as you do like me but you're afraid of what could happen if you allowed yourself to be vulnerable."

I feel myself being pulled away from my own armor. I need to steer this conversation back to him. I've never been put in this position before; it's unnerving. "I want to take things slow," I say, knowing Ben is enough of a gentleman that he'll respect my reply enough to leave it alone.

He blinks several times while staring at me before returning his attention to his food. "Do you like my lasagna?"

Thankfully he's backed off. "I do; it's very good." I take a few more mouthfuls. "Tell me about your job." I need to piece together who's wanting him dead and, more so, who's feeding the bank account with millions of untouched dollars.

"Not much to tell." A part of me can sense he's hiding something.

Our conversation stays light, but my brain is constantly on alert trying to pick up any scrap of information he may unwittingly drop.

Is he a dirty cop? Is he on the take and now he's an inconvenience for whoever's been paying him? One way or another, I'm going to find out.

CHAPTER SIX

─ • ─

I sit on the edge of my bed and roll my neck from side to side. Standing, I stretch my arms over my head attempting to wake myself up. Today, I have research to do on Ethan Martelli before I call to meet with him.

I make myself a coffee and as I'm walking over to the sofa, I put my earpiece in and call Agent.

"Hey, boss. How's hit one-four-nine going?"

"Hit one-four-nine? As in one hundred and forty-nine?"

"Yep, Ben Pearson. Have you killed him yet?"

"I've killed more than a hundred and forty-nine people, Agent."

"Yes, you have, but he'll be your hundred and forty-ninth *paid* hit."

"Remind me to give you more work. Apparently, you have way too much time on your hands."

"You're avoiding the question, 15. Have you killed him yet?"

I arch a brow and shake my head. Opening my laptop, I bring it to life and reply, "I need you to get me back into the police personnel records."

I hear him tapping on his keyboard. The screen on my computer opens into the database. "Easy," he proudly announces.

"Bring up any bank records you can find on Ethan Martelli." While Agent is tapping away silently, I read over Ethan's personnel file. I snort with a small chuckle as I read his colorful career. "He's twenty-nine," I say to myself. Ethan has been on the police force for nine years and has a string of complaints against him. "Interesting." I read how numerous complaints have been filed about his anger issues. I also notice the police department has done nothing to manage those anger issues. "Hang on." I click into a restricted file that shows he actually has had disciplinary action taken against him. He was suspended, though after only a handful of days, it was lifted and he returned to work with full pay. He's also somehow managed to skip every second ranking.

"Open another window," Agent instructs. "This is what I've found."

"Thanks." I hang up on Agent and sit staring at the accounts he's found. Ethan has four accounts, each with over two hundred thousand in them. Not one withdrawal from any of the accounts. Not for gas, utilities, food or anything. How bizarre. "Who are you, Ethan Martelli?" I ask as I glance at the time on the corner of my laptop. "Shit."

Standing, I head back into my bedroom and search for the card he gave me with his number. I pick my phone up and dial his number. "Anna," he answers on the second ring. I didn't give him my number, but a man like Ethan Martelli is going to do his own research on me. "I'm pleased you called."

I roll my eyes at his fakeness. "Of course, Ethan. We do have a date today, unless you forgot?" I say in a sickening saccharine voice.

"How's lunch? I'll come and pick you up at eleven-thirty." He's trying to figure out where I'm staying so he has the upper hand in this toxic and dangerous game of cat-and-mouse we're playing.

"I need to head into town anyway, so I'll meet you."

"I'm happy to be your chauffeur."

Fucker. I know what he's doing because this is exactly what I'd do too. "Or I could pick you up?" I offer with a smirk.

"How about we meet at Mamma's? Do you know where that is?"

"I'll find it."

"Eleven-thirty?"

"Sounds good." I glance at the time again and know I'll be cutting it short. "See you then, Ethan." I hang up and find myself pacing back and forth in my room. I'll need to get Agent to look into him further, but for now, I have to get ready to meet him.

As I fly down the road toward Mamma's, I can't help but laugh when I see the police car pull in behind me. I glance in my mirror and know it's Ethan. He used the vast, overgrown, tree-lined road to cloak his vehicle and wait for me. "Smart," I say as I up the speed and push boundaries.

It appears Ethan Martelli may actually be a worthy adversary. *We'll see.* Now this is going to be fun.

As it turns out, Mamma's is a small restaurant on the other side of town. I pull up outside, and Ethan parks directly behind me. I get out and lock my car. "Were you following me?" I ask and add a pathetic giggle.

"You were speeding, Miss Moore."

"Oops, was I?" I bring my hand up to cover my gaping mouth. "Is that why you were following me?"

"It's simply coincidence."

I really want to get to the root of who he is, but this is also kind of fun. Letting him think I'm no one when in actual fact I could put him down within seconds. He opens the door to Mamma's for me and stands quite close to me as we wait for the hostess. I'm not even surprised to see my old friend Plastic Tammy. "Oh hi," she says as she sees me.

"Hi, Tammy. You work here too?" I ask with a smile.

"Yeah. The diner is closed two days a week, and I work here those two days." She smiles broadly. She glances at Ethan and her brows draw together. "Hi, Ethan," she adds, voice breaking slightly. Tammy's cheeks turn pink and when she glances at me, I notice her eyes have reddened.

"Tammy," he replies coldly with a sharp nod. *What an ass.*

"Would you like a table?"

"We sure would," I answer and offer her a smile.

"This way." She picks up two menus and walks toward one of the handful of empty tables. She places the menus on the table and takes a small step back. Without looking at Ethan again she says, "I'm also your server today so I'll be back in a few moments to take your order."

"Thank you, Tammy," I say as I pull the chair out and sit. Ethan slides a menu over to me as Tammy turns to walk away. "Did you break that poor girl's heart?"

Ethan becomes rigid and looks over his shoulder toward Tammy. "No, we just know each other from high school."

Does he honestly believe I'm going to fall for his lies? "High school? Really?" I ask as I play with the corner of my menu.

"Yeah, she was in the year behind me."

I know the words he's speaking are nothing but lies, considering I've already looked into his personnel file. "Did you grow up here?" Besides, I would've known him from when I lived here.

"Yeah, my entire life." His lies are mounting. "I love Bankstown Creek, it's my home."

My phone vibrates in my pocket and take it out to look at. A text message appears and I smirk at it. "Are you ready to order?" Tammy appears and asks.

"Do you know what you want, Anna?" Ethan asks.

"Not yet, but you order." I bring my phone up and open the text message. I want to laugh out loud when I see someone sneak up between Ethan's police cruiser and my car and fit a tracker under the trunk of my car. I close out of the app and place my phone face down on the table. "Sorry about that, I got a text from one of my employees."

Ethan narrows his eyes suspiciously at me. He looks to my menu and back to me. "What would you like?"

The first thing I see on the menu sounds delicious "Pho please, and can I have a bottle of water, unopened please."

"Unopened?" Ethan questions. "I'll have the chicken and wild rice burger and a soda." He picks both our menus up and hands them to Tammy. She looks hurt by his disinterested behavior, but she takes our menus and walks away. "So, why unopened?"

"I've watched enough police and crime shows to know you never accept an opened drink from anyone. As a cop, you should know that," I tease as I add a laugh for plausibility.

He looks around the restaurant before turning his attention back to me. "You were telling me about what you do." He shifts in his seat rather rigidly.

My senses heighten as I watch him shift his gaze from me to outside. "I'm a headhunter for big businesses," I launch into the public story he's likely already found.

"Sounds interesting. What's the process with headhunting?"

The corner of my mouth draws up as I control my laughter at his blatant attempt to trip me up. "I get a lead, and chase the person down until I find them." Yeah, that pretty much sums it up.

"How successful are you at your job?"

"I always get my man," I reply with a tinge of snark.

"Your drinks." Tammy places my unopened water and Ethan's soda on the table. "Your food shouldn't be too long." Tammy still hasn't looked at Ethan.

I watch as she walks away, and I lean over the table toward Ethan. "She hasn't been able to look at you. What happened?"

"I told you, nothing. We went to school together." Ethan's jaw tenses. "I've never given her the time of day, I mean, look at her." He tilts his head to the side and rolls his eyes.

What a condescending asshole. "You're right, she's way too good for you," I say basking in my own cockiness.

He arrogantly laughs out loud. "Tell me about yourself, Anna. What makes Anna Moore get out of bed every morning?"

He's trying to analyze me, and I fucking hate this bullshit. "Headhunting." I gloat with a grin.

"You love your work? That's good."

"The thrill of the chase makes my heart flutter and my blood pump harder through my veins. Tell me about you, *Ethan Martelli.*"

Ethan's phone begins to vibrate on the table, and I glimpse down at it. "Sorry, I need to take this." He lifts his phone and stands to walk away from the table. I already know what's going to happen. He's going to return and tell me there's been an emergency and he has to leave. He's the one who had someone sneak up to my car and fit a tracking device to it, and now that it's done he doesn't actually need to be here. This lunch was nothing but a ruse, a ploy to get me here because he wants to know everything about me, starting with where I'm staying. He returns to his seat and hails Tammy. "I'm sorry, I need to go. Family emergency, you understand," he says to me.

"Of course. Nothing comes before family."

"Rain check?" He looks over his shoulder and calls Tammy again.

"I'll be in town for a while and I'm sure we'll cross paths again," I cryptically reply.

Tammy returns and looks between us. "Your food shouldn't be too much longer," she says anticipating why he's beckoned her over.

"We're sorry, Tammy, but we need to leave."

"No, I'll stay. You go ahead. I'm hungry," I say.

Ethan looks as if he expected a different answer from me. He scratches his chin before giving both Tammy and me a short smile. "Great." Ethan's jaw loosens as his power move to have me tracked fades.

"I won't be long behind you. I'll just eat and go home," I say, throwing him a bone and giving him false hope that he still has a chance of finding out where I live.

Ethan opens his mouth, but he's clearly at a loss for words because he closes it again, smiles, and turns to leave. I look to Tammy who shrugs and walks away.

The moment my food arrives I inhale it because I'm hungry. I pay the check and return to my car. I have no idea what type of tracking device was fitted to my car, so I'm careful to turn my phone off so it can't be listened to or tracked. I guess I better get myself over to a busy mall.

I drive straight to one of the biggest malls, one county over from Bankstown Creek, and pull up between two cars. I look around to make sure no one has followed me or sees me. I duck behind my car and feel for the tracking device. I manage to locate it easily and shake my head at how clumsy these people are. They have no idea who they're dealing with.

Effortlessly, I attach the tracking device to the car next to mine, then stand and dust off my knees. I get back into my car and head out before they figure out what I've done.

The moment I'm back at the cabin, I place my earpiece in and dial Agent. "Is this my favorite assassin calling?"

"I need you to find out as much as you can about Ethan Martelli."

"Anything specific I should be searching for?" his tone alters to more businesslike.

"Anything you find on him, I want to know."

"Did something happen?"

"Yeah, he tried to covertly fit my car with a tracking device."

Agent snorts. "Oh man…" He clicks his tongue to the roof of his mouth. "Are you going to allow him to have an open casket or will you do enough damage that it'll have to be closed casket?"

"How long will it take you to find out everything?" I ask as I gloss over his ridiculous question.

"I should have something within the next day or two. It really depends what I find as I dig around."

"Get it to me ASAP." I hang up and take my earpiece out as I head into the kitchen to grab a bottle of water from the fridge. My phone vibrates on the counter, and as I'm unscrewing the lid I look at the message that's come through.

Dinner tomorrow night.

I find myself smiling as I look at the message. I shouldn't reply, nor should I be excited about seeing Ben. **Sure.**

I'll have something delicious for you.

"Oh, really, Mr. Pearson," I say as I catch myself smiling even wider. **I'll be there by six.**

Can't wait.

I place my phone on the counter and stand staring at it without seeing it for a long time. I have to kill Ben, so why the hell am I agreeing to have dinner with him? "Three million," I say to myself. "He's worth three million dollars." I back away from the counter and rub at the tension forming under my brows. "Three million," I repeat as I put distance between me and the phone.

That's exactly what I need to do. I need to kill him and then walk away.

Yep, that's precisely what I'm going to do.

So why does it feel like the weight of the world is resting on my chest?

CHAPTER SEVEN

— ◦ —

I had a shit sleep. I tossed and turned for nearly the entire night. No sooner would I close my eyes, then I'd startle awake, making it harder to go back to sleep. I think I caught about an hour of broken sleep while the rest of the time, I kept thinking about Ben and what I could do to make it look like an accident.

I'm about to turn into his driveway, and I feel sick to my stomach. I'm going to have to kill him soon, but first I need to turn these stupid emotions off. I turn my car off and take a moment to bury what I'm feeling. I can't let this cloud my mind. I have a job to do.

A knocking on my window forces me to lift my chin. Ben's standing by my door with a massive smile. "Why are you sitting out here?" he asks through the glass. I grab my phone before I open the door and slide out of the car. Ben has me in a tight embrace. "I've missed you," he whispers and places a soft and gentle kiss to my cheek.

I feel myself stiffen at his overtly affectionate embrace. *He's a target, a hit, that's it.* "I'm hungry," I spill to avoid his warmth.

"I've cooked for you," he proudly announces. "Tell me about your day." Ben wraps his arm around my shoulders and snuggles in to kiss my temple. "Have you found a house to buy yet?"

"I've looked at a couple of houses, but nothing has caught my attention yet. I also almost had lunch with Ethan yesterday.

Ben's hand flexes around my shoulder as we reach his front door. He quickly pulls himself together, releases his grip on me, and opens the door. "Yeah?" his taut voice reveals his opinion about that. "Ethan didn't tell me."

Why would he? "I think Ethan is suspicious of me."

"Of you? Why would he be?"

Ben pushes his hand into mine and links our fingers together as he leads me toward the kitchen. "I have no idea. But you know what I found interesting?"

"What's that?" Ben effortlessly drifts around the kitchen.

"We were at Mamma's and Tammy was the server. I couldn't help but notice how she reacted to seeing him."

"That's because they were seeing one another," he says. He stops and turns to look at me. "I think I'd best speak with Ethan about you."

"About me?" I ask, genuinely surprised.

"Yes, I'm not fond of him asking you out for lunch, or dinner, or any other activity."

How cute. "I can handle myself when it comes to unwanted attention."

Ben stops preparing the food and turns toward me. He thrusts his chest out while his jaw tightens. "Ethan Martelli isn't someone I want you spending time with."

This is new, something I haven't experienced before. "Are you jealous?"

Ben's lips slightly part as he attempts not to stare at me. He slightly shakes his head and returns to finish the preparation of our dinner. There's something about his silence that's quite arousing to me. He *is* jealous. "No," he finally replies in a small hoarse croak. "I'm not jealous, but I don't trust him and I don't want him near you."

I'm not even sure why he feels so protective of me, but I'm pleased by it. My smile is naturally large as I stare at him. "You know you're cute when you get like that?"

"Cute?" his tone changes to become more playful. "Did you call me cute?"

I try my hardest to hold in my smile. "I did," I counter with sass. "This whole neanderthal thing is quite endearing."

"Neanderthal?"

"Are you going to keep repeating everything I say? Because that'll be annoying." I pointedly look to Ben.

His lips break into a massive smirk. "Set the dining room table," he orders.

"Bossy much?" I push off the stool at the kitchen island and walk around to be in the kitchen beside him. I start opening the cupboards to find plates, and also to see if there's anything in them that might give me some insight as to why someone wants him dead. As I turn, I see Ben smiling and talking to himself. I don't know what comes over me, but I stalk toward him and push his shoulder so I'm standing in front of him. I slide my fingers through his hair and pull him down to kiss me. He drops his knife to the counter with a clatter and grabs my hips.

A small groan vibrates through him as we play this erotic duel of nibbling and licking. God, I want him. He breaks the devouring kiss and steps backward. "I want a kiss like that every time I see you, Anna."

My stomach knots at the tormented reality that Ben's days are num-bered. Suddenly, the hair at the back of neck stands to attention as a blanket of cold cascades slowly over my body. My adrenaline jumps while I attempt to discover where the danger is coming from. There's a knock on the door, and I suck in a breath. With my shoulders back, I head straight for the door.

Something is wrong.

Ben beats me to the door and opens it. "Good evening, sir, I'm wondering if you're happy with your current cable provider?" There's something wrong with this. I can feel it in my stomach. The guy flicks a hard glance over to me, then back to Ben.

I step forward and look up and down the street. The van parked down the street looks out of place, wrong. "Sorry, what did you say your name is and where are you from?"

He wrings his hands together before becoming unnaturally stiff. "I'm sorry," he starts with a forced smile. "My name is Simon and I'm from Cablevision. We're going door to door today, checking that everyone is happy with their cable provider." His left eye twitches as he attempts to regain control of the situation.

"We're very happy with our provider," I say. "Enjoy your day." I close the door on him.

"We barely ever get door-to-door people," Ben says casually.

"They must be trying to drum up new business." Without Ben noticing, I turn to look over my shoulder out the front window. I see the cable guy get in the van and leave, but there's no tag on the back of the van for me to memorize.

There's something definitely wrong with this picture.

"I hope you're hungry." Ben makes quick work of setting the table, which I was supposed to do.

"Starving." I'm on high alert though. I can't help but keep scanning the environment for any possible danger.

"What would you like to drink? I have wine, or soda, or..."

"Just water, thank you." I need to keep my focus sharp in case Simon returns with reinforcements. Ben returns to the table with a pitcher of ice water, then brings over the food. There's breaded chicken, sides of garlic mushrooms, corn on the cob and green beans. "Looks good," I say as I carefully scan everywhere. "Tell me about your parents," I start, already knowing they were killed by a drunk driver.

"My parents both died in the same accident just over six years ago." He places a massive piece of chicken on my plate, then hands me the mushrooms. "They were returning from Emily's wedding, and..." He looks down at his empty plate and slightly shrugs. "I miss them," he candidly admits.

I lean across the table and place my hand over his and give it a gentle squeeze. "That's a shit way to go. I'm sorry."

He looks up and offers me a troubled smile. "Thank you."

I retract my arm and pick up the flatware beside the plate. "So, I did some mild stalking of you, and saw you had given an interview about a drug haul you and your team intercepted."

He cocks a brow and tilts his head to the side. "Mild stalking?"

I hold up my hand and with my thumb and finger to indicate about an inch in size. "Just a little stalking, nothing too over the top." I laugh internally. I know more about him than he wants me to. "In the interview you said you had intel that it was a shipment of guns, but it turned out it was cocaine and crystal meth."

"Yep." Ben smiles proudly.

"How could you get it so wrong?" I tease as I pop some of the chicken in my mouth.

He stares at me and slightly shakes his head. "I have a CI—a confidential informant—who I've been working with for a while. She told me it was a shipment of automatic and semi-automatic weapons, but it turned out to be drugs instead."

"No weapons then?"

"No weapons." He cuts his chicken and takes a bite. "This informant has never given me bad intel in the past."

"A shipment of drugs is not bad intel, Ben."

"No, it's not," he says with a hint of disappointment. "I would've preferred the guns."

So would I. "Does your informant work with the gun runners?"

"My informant is so private she's completely cloaked. The department doesn't know anything about her, nor does anyone at the station."

"No paper trail?"

"God, no. She'd be dead if anyone found out she works with me." He looks down at his food for a few seconds. "Getting the drugs off the streets was a good feeling, but I really wanted the guns."

Me too. "Drugs are the bane of our existence," I say. "I have no sympathy for drug dealers who are caught, or better still, killed."

Ben smirks as he chews. "That's quite cold, Anna."

I half shrug. "Well, it's my truth. I don't give a rat's ass what happens to a drug dealer. They cause too much havoc in the world."

"But arms dealers you're okay with?"

This is a catch twenty-two. I have to be careful how to respond to this so I don't give away any part of my identity. "That's an entirely different situation."

"Why? Arms dealers can cause more havoc than drugs."

"Drugs are addictive."

"Guns in the wrong hands can be too," he argues. "A Desert Tech MDR can do more damage than a low-level drug dealer who's cut the shit out of a product with other poisons and sold it to some poor bastard."

I wet my bottom lip when he mentions the assault rifle. "A what?" I ask with a small voice break.

"A Desert Tech MDR." I can't take my eyes off his mouth. "It's an American assault weapon."

"It is?" My pulse jumps with anticipation.

"It is."

I push the chair back, and walk over to where Ben is sitting. "There's something sexy when you talk about guns." I push my fingers through his hair and yank his head back. I lower until my mouth is on his.

"Remington," he whispers against my mouth as he pushes his chair out.

Straddling his hips, I can feel his erection growing rapidly. "I like that." I move my hips to find that delicious friction between us.

"Sig," he mumbles as he frantically pulls my t-shirt off over my head. He effortlessly pushes the plates off of the table, the stoneware and food falling to the carpet, then stands while picking me up with his hands under my thighs. He lays me on the table and kisses down between my cleavage. "I'm so hungry and thirsty," he says as he bites and licks his way down to the top of my jeans. Standing, he grabs his t-shirt and tears it off over his head. Mr. Ben Pearson has a sexy tattoo of a shattered skull with a gun pointing at it and smoke drifting up from the barrel of it. "Take these off." He flicks the waist band of my jeans.

"You don't have to ask me twice." I make quick work of taking my jeans off.

Ben grabs his chair and brings it forward. "I'm so thirsty." He leans down and strokes his tongue through my pussy. Grabbing my legs, he lifts them over his shoulders as he plunges his tongue into me.

"Oh, God," I murmur as I close my eyes.

"You taste like fucking bliss." Ben's hands slide under my ass as he scoots me closer to him. "I want you to come on my face."

I lean up on one elbow to watch him feast on me. Tangling my fingers through his hair, I roughly pull him toward me as he uses his mouth and tongue energetically. Our eyes meet and he watches me as I watch him fucking me with his mouth. He sits back slightly, giving me the best view of his wet mouth. "You're not done yet," I say as I urge his head forward. I let go of his head and rub at my clit. "Of course, I could finish this without you," I tease.

He smacks my hand away and cocks an eyebrow. "This is mine to take care of." He lowers his head again to lick, slurp and suck on my pussy. "So good," he mumbles.

I can't take my eyes off him as he flicks his tongue, bringing me to the edge. "Keep going." I roll my head back, engulfed in the feeling of what his tongue is doing.

"Watch me," he demands.

I open my eyes and sit up straighter, resting on my elbows. Ben reaches to grab my breast. His hand squeezes as he keeps fucking me with his mouth while watching me. "That's it." My hips buck forward on their own, impaling myself further on his tongue. "Right there." I gyrate as I use Ben's face for my own satisfaction. "There, yes, keep that going."

He smiles as he continues to plunge his tongue into me. Ben sucks my clit into his mouth before flicking it several times. My hips ride his face as he strokes and thrusts his tongue into me. He rises, breathless, and says, "Come on my face, baby girl."

As he resumes his attentions, my body inches closer and closer to release. My heartbeat is spiraling out of control as I'm about to come. Closing my eyes for one last time, the whirlwind bubbling inside me erupts with a long, low groan. My back arches, my hips slow and I lie back, opening my eyes. Ben pulls away and wipes at his mouth. "Thank you," I say as I catch my breath.

"No, thank you. I thoroughly enjoy having your cum on my face. I could easily get used to this." I lower my legs and finally sit up to look for my jeans. I scoot off the dining table, grab my panties and jeans before searching for my t-shirt. "I think you should stay with me tonight so I have access to your body," Ben casually says as he too shrugs into his t-shirt.

Realization falls over me. I shouldn't have let him do that. "I can't," I say as I look toward the door, ready to make a quick exit.

"I think you can but you don't want to."

"Exactly," my voice is thick with regret. "I shouldn't have let it get this far." I can't let this cloud my judgment. I know what I have to do. With a tight ache in my chest, I head toward the door. "Thank you for dinner." I reach for the door handle, but Ben turns me and traps me between his hard and heated body and the door.

"You can't go." He leans into me and kisses my forehead. My aroma on his face is going to send me over the edge. "Stay." He cages me between his arms. "Please."

I can't think straight when I'm with him. No other man has ever affected me the way Ben has. The longer I stay here, the harder it'll be to end his life. He trails his nose down my cheek before kissing below my ear. "I have to go," I whisper as I gather my resolve and place my hands on his chest to slightly push him back.

He takes a small step backward and stares into my eyes. "You *can* stay."

I lower my head and wet my lips. Shaking my head, I don't look up at him; instead, I turn, open the door, and walk out. I'm in my car and out of his driveway before he has a chance to find his car keys.

I know now I'm developing feelings for him. This is more than just sexual attraction. I need to go back to my stone-cold self. I smash my hand on the steering wheel several times in anger. "Fuck!" I yell as I take my speed up.

I catch a look in the rearview mirror and see the van falling in behind me.

Suddenly, all my frustration is replaced by anger. That fucker is after me and not Ben. I slow enough to try and see if there's any tag on the front of the car, but of course there isn't.

Traffic is light, which makes losing him a little harder, but that's okay. I know these streets like the back of my hand from thirteen years ago. My phone is constantly ringing, and I know it's Ben trying to connect with me. But I can't deal with or even think about Ben at the moment. My sole focus is on the van following me. With some tricky turns and careful maneuvering, I lose the van easily.

I'm overly cautious as I drive back to the cabin to make sure I'm not followed. I run a quick security check on the cabin once I pull up out in front of it and when I'm satisfied I've had no breaches, I leave my car and head inside.

The messages from Ben are relentless, as are the voicemails.

I need to rein in my emotions and deal with the bigger problem at hand.

Who does Simon from Cablevision work for? And what do they want with me?

I'll find out and I'll end them.

Slowly and painfully.

CHAPTER EIGHT

S omething more is happening here in Bankstown Creek. What I know is Ethan had a tracking device placed on my car, and Simon from Cablevision followed me.

Are they related?

Or could Simon be attempting to collect on the bounty Ronan Murphy had put on my head from back when I was fifteen? He knew I was going to come after him. So Ronan set a bounty on my head, hoping someone would take me out before I got to him. I pace back and forth in the kitchen as I try to find the connections between everyone.

It all may be unrelated, or it's all connected. I pop my earpiece in and dial Agent. "You're up bright and early."

"Have you found anything about Ethan Martelli yet?"

"I haven't been able to find anything on him, which is surprising considering my mad skills at hacking. However, I did have a look into the employer who hired you for this hit."

"What did you find?"

"Anthony Mancini," he says.

Shit, Anthony Mancini. I blow out a caught breath and lean against the counter. "Are you sure?"

"When have I ever been wrong?"

I hang up and take my earpiece out. I stand for a moment staring at nothing. "Fuck!" I yell and throw my arm out to knock the closest thing off the kitchen counter. I stand staring at the toaster I've violently swiped to the floor and take a deep breath. "Fuck," I grumble as I pick it up. Anthony Mancini is heavily protected by a small army. His reach is long into drugs, prostitution, human trafficking, arms dealing, and everything in between. He's the mob boss covering the entire East Coast and a considerable distance into the Midwest. If needed, getting to Anthony will be harder than getting to Ronan was, but thankfully, not impossible. He'll be on a par with the president I assassinated a few years ago. For now, I have to push Anthony Mancini to the side and try to figure out what is going on here in Bankstown Creek.

My mind is spinning at a million miles an hour, though. Why would Anthony Mancini want Ben dead? Is Ben close to a break in one of Anthony's operations? None of this makes sense.

I walk into my bedroom to search for my civilian phone and pick it up. Ben has called and left several messages for me. Sitting on the edge of the bed, I dial his number. "I'm sorry for yesterday, I came on too strong," he says.

I lift my hand and rub at the tension across my forehead. "We need to talk," I say without acknowledging his apology.

"Do you want to come here for lunch?"

"No," I reply with haste and eagerness. I can't have Simon show up and attempt to kill me while I'm at Ben's. We need to be somewhere public so I can keep Ben safe. Safe until I figure out what's happening; and then I can kill him.

"Um, okay," Ben replies with hurt in his voice.

I can't apologize for the way I am. "We can meet at the diner you like, or at Mamma's. I don't care; either one is fine for me."

There's a second of hesitation. "We can meet at Mamma's, but first I need to have my weapon inspected and signed off that I didn't discharge a round while I was on vacation."

"Police do that?" I asked, genuinely surprised.

"It's something I introduced when I became chief of police because I didn't want rogue cops thinking they could discharge service weapons for any unofficial reasons. I can be there by noon," there's another pause, like he wants to add something to the end of that.

"Noon works for me."

"Looking forward to it."

I hang up and place the phone beside me. What exactly am I going to tell him? Maybe it's best I get this over with, then I can leave Bankstown Creek and return to my normal life. But that still leaves so many unanswered questions, and I refuse to run from cocky assholes who think they can take me out.

Although I know about Anthony Mancini professionally, I'm not too familiar with his private life. We've never crossed paths before so I've never really needed to look into him. I go to my laptop and begin researching. The dark web has a library of information, it's a matter of rifling through the trash and piecing together facts. "Who are you?"

Anthony has been married for thirty-one years to a bombshell of a woman named Gabriella. They have two sons, one of whom died nearly eleven years ago in a gun-related incident. I find the name of the son who died, but I can't find anything on the other son.

The time on the bottom right-hand corner of my laptop screen catches my attention, and I know I need to get ready for my lunch date with Ben. I still don't know what I'm going to say to him, but I guess I'll figure that out when I get there.

After a quick shower, I dress in jeans and a t-shirt and tie my long, dark hair up in a ponytail. I slide the keys to my car off the counter and head out to it.

The drive into town has me hyperaware of every car around me. A part of me is waiting for Ethan to pop out of nowhere, or even Simon in the Cablevision van. However, by the time I pull up outside of Mamma's, I've declared the entire trip uneventful. I slide out of the driver's seat and head into the restaurant.

I can see Ben sitting toward the back. I quickly scan the restaurant to find we're actually the only ones in here other than the waitstaff. The moment I walk through the door, Ben is already on his feet and making his way toward me. He wraps me in a hug and kisses the side of my head. "Thank you for coming today." He pulls back and guides me over to our table with his hand to the small of my back.

"I wouldn't miss it," I reply. Ben pulls my chair out and waits for me to be seated before he sits beside me. His left leg is brushing up against my right leg as he reaches for my hand.

"About yesterday—" he starts.

We're interrupted by Tammy who places two menus on the table. "Hey, Ben." She smiles broadly at him. "Hi," she greets me with equal enthusiasm. "You're back." Tammy places the menus on the table.

"The food is good here," I say as I casually peruse the menu.

"Just holler when you're ready. As you can see, you're my first customers for the day." Tammy effectively turns to leave us alone.

"About yesterday," Ben starts again. "I'm sorry for making you feel so uncomfortable that you felt you had to leave." Ben plays with my fingertips as he looks down to avoid my eyes.

I swallow the lump in my throat. "I'll be leaving Bankstown Creek tomorrow," I say with absolutely no conviction.

"What? Why?"

I need to pull myself together and get this damn job done before I develop any more feelings for him. "Because I have a business I need take care of, and the longer I stay here, the harder it is for me to do the work. Besides, I haven't been successful in finding a vacation home, so I'm going to shelve that for now and maybe something will come up in the future."

Ben's shoulders fall forward and he clears his throat. "Can we talk about this?"

"There's nothing to talk about, Ben. I have a job to do, and I can't stay here." The pain in my chest tightens with the reality of what I'm going to do tonight. It's best I get this over and done with. Ben Pearson was only ever supposed to be a one-night stand, not a long-term commitment. Especially considering I'm going to kill him tonight. I'll break into his house when he's sleeping, and put two bullets in his head. It'll be quick, painless, and he won't even know what's hit him.

"How about we order some food and talk about this?"

If these are the last moments I ever get to spend with Ben, then I'll draw this lunch out for as long as I can. "I'd like that." I offer him the only comfort I can give him, a genuine smile. My stomach is twisting with worry, though.

Ben turns to summon Tammy. She picks up her tablet and begins to walk over to us.

The hair on the back of my neck stands to attention, as a layer of ice enshrouds my body. Danger is near. I can feel it.

I look to the door, then back to Tammy. Her smile instantly disappears and her eyes widen. She collapses to the floor in front of us. My gun is in the glove compartment of my car, not on me. There's no echo from the shot, just a small popping sound. I jump to my feet to run out, but Ben knocks me backward. There's another small pop and the bullet flies past my head. There's one more, louder pop, distinctly different from the first two. Again, I fly up to my feet and I see the gunman lying prone just inside the door. Ben's standing protectively in front of me.

The dead gunman on the floor is Simon. Beside him is his weapon, fitted with a silencer. Ben kicks out of reach.

"Are you okay?" Ben asks as he turns and checks me over. He runs his hands through my hair and closely inspects me. "Are you shot? Hurt anywhere?" Ben kisses my forehead. "I know this is scary."

Scary...right. My only regret is not having my gun on me and taking that fucker out myself. "I'm okay," I reply with a quiver in my voice. I have to hide my true self and play a distraught, innocent bystander here.

With one arm wrapped around my shoulder, he digs into his pocket and removes his phone. I watch as he dials the station. As he relays the information, I look at Tammy lying lifelessly on the ground. I feel sorry for her because she truly was harmless and didn't deserve to die in such a cold way.

Once Ben is off the phone, he guides me over to a seat and lowers me. He kneels in front of me and rubs his hands up and down my arms. I've never been good at projecting vulnerability, but I have to right now so I don't reveal myself. I try to muster some tears, but tears aren't my thing. "Don't look at her, something like that sears into your memory and I don't want you having the nightmares that come from seeing someone dead."

Nightmares? Please. I'll sleep like a log and never think of it again. My armor and mask need to be firmly in place. "It's so horrible," I whisper as I look away from Tammy. In all fairness though, I really do feel bad for her.

I hear the police sirens closing in on our location. The cars pull up with a screech outside the restaurant and Ethan is the first one in the door with his weapon drawn. Our eyes connect and he flinches. He shakes his head, narrowing his eyes at me. I can't help but lift the corner of my lip in a slight smirk.

"Ethan," Ben says as he abruptly stands and heads over to him.

Ethan stares at me for a hard second before moving his focus to Ben. He now knows I removed the tracker, which means he knows I'm more than he thought I was. Good, I like it when people underestimate me. It makes killing them all the more fun.

"What happened?" Ethan asks Ben.

"We were about to order when that guy killed Tammy then aimed his weapon at us." Ben intakes a sharp breath and shakes his head. "I had to take him down."

Ethan has his own mask in place. He looks around and runs his hand through his hair. "Anyone else hurt?"

I look over toward the kitchen where the three kitchen staff have now gathered out from behind the host counter, looking at the dead bodies. "No, only Tammy and this guy," Ben says as he pointedly looks to Simon from Cablevision. Ben squats in front of the guy and furrows his brows, then turns and looks at me. Yep, he's figured out that Simon from Cablevision *isn't* from Cablevision.

"Do you know this guy?" Ethan asks when he sees Ben's reaction.

"No, I don't."

"Anna, do you know him?"

"I can't say that I do," I reply.

Ethan's cold demeanor is an obvious tell that he's certainly not who he says he is. "I'll take Anna back to the station to get a statement from her," Ethan offers.

"I can drive myself." This asshole wants me alone in a car with him.

"I think it's a good idea if you go with Ethan. Shock might set in while you're driving, and I don't want you hurt." *Shock? Me?*

I lean in and give Ben a kiss on the cheek. "Yeah, you're right." I look up into his piercing eyes and smile. He really is a good guy, which makes killing him even harder. But I have a job I've been paid to do.

Ethan is waiting for me by the door. I turn my head to the side as I walk past the dead body, pretending I can't look at him. Hell, I would've preferred to torture him a bit before putting a bullet through him. "Have I ever told you I really like your car, Anna?" Ethan says as we walk toward his police cruiser.

"Thank you, Ethan." I smile sweetly at him. He opens the back door of the cruiser and waits for me to get in. "Am I under arrest?"

"No, why?" He wants me in the back because there he can control me. He can lock me in and attempt an interrogation. I side step the open back door and get into the front passenger side. Ethan slams the back door with too much force and walks around to the driver's seat. He slides in and closes the door. "What were you doing with Ben?" he finally asks once he pulls out onto the road.

I roll my eyes and sigh. "We were at a restaurant, Ethan, which means we were there to eat."

"You've been seeing Ben quite a lot."

I let out a long breath along with a low groan. "Really?" I look over to him and shake my head in annoyance. "You have me all alone in the car with no listening devices and you're questioning me about Ben?" I scrunch my mouth and widen my eyes with sarcasm. "I thought a man of your caliber would be asking me the questions you know I won't answer once we're inside the station."

Ethan's knuckles tighten around the wheel. A vein traveling down the column of his neck protrudes as he tightens his jaw. Oh, this is fun. "Who are you, Anna Moore?"

"Meh, boring."

"What questions do you suggest I ask?" He grinds his teeth.

I look over to him and snicker. "You want me to do your job?" I taunt.

"What are you doing in Bankstown Creek?"

I let my head roll back and dribble an incoherent sound. "Boring."

"What are you doing with Ben?"

I clap my hands and sit straighter. "Enjoying myself."

"Why are you in Bankstown Creek?"

"Great, back to the boring questions."

"Where do you live?"

"Seriously?" I can see I'm getting under his skin and he's on the verge of breaking, which of course will make my job of finding out who he really is much easier. "We both know you did a background check on me."

"You're really pissing me off, lady." He stomps on the brakes as he pulls over onto the shoulder. This is going to get interesting so much faster than I anticipated.

My phone starts ringing in my pocket, and I take it out just as the car skids to a stop. I answer it before Ethan has a chance to knock it out of my hands. "Hey, Ben. Give me a second Ethan's slammed on the brakes and pulled the car over for some reason."

"What? Why's he pulled the car over?"

"I'm not sure. Here, you can talk to him." I know he can easily smash the phone, but what Ethan doesn't know is I can kill him within a heartbeat. I hand the phone over to Ethan. "Ben wants to talk to you." I'm having the time of my life badgering Ethan.

He snatches the phone out of my hand and holds it up to his ear. "Hey." He listens while carefully watching me. "I thought I hit an animal," his voice says one thing, but his rigid jaw and hard eyes says he wants to hurt me. "Sure." He lowers the phone from his ear, checks that the call has been disconnected, then slides it into the pocket of his shirt. He pulls back onto the road and takes the steering wheel in a death grip. "You're going to tell me everything about you, because we both know your background check came up with fuck-all information. I know whatever I found has been planted there to make you look like you're some kind of fucking normal person. But we both know you're not who you say you are."

I lift my hand to my chest and whimper—with a grin. "What are you saying, Ethan? I'm so hurt." Teasing him is the highlight of my day. Even better than seeing the fake Cablevision guy dead. "You need to learn to read the room. You seriously suck at it."

"Did you remove the tracking device from your car?"

"Finally, a semi-decent question. Of course, I removed it. I'm not a fan of people tracking me. I'm not an animal."

"You're not a headhunter, either. So what do you do?"

I cross my arms in front of my chest and groan again. "You are the worst at asking questions. Do you really call this an interrogation?"

Suddenly, his left hand balls into a fist and he turns and smashes into my shoulder. "Answer me!" he yells.

I don't even flinch. "Anger management obviously didn't work, but smart move, Ethan. Hitting me where it won't show. Ethan one, Anna zero. It's okay, I'll settle the score." I've given him a little hint that I've been doing research of my own on him.

"Are you in Bankstown Creek for a reason?"

"Yep."

"What's the reason?"

"To buy a house." One little smack isn't going to get me to talk.

"I want to know who comes into my town because I'm protective of everyone and everything here."

He's just given me the biggest clue. *Everyone and everything*. That means something is here that he doesn't want anyone to discover. Ethan pulls up in front of the police station and I'm out of the car before he even has a chance to turn it off. I look back over my shoulder as I enter the station and give him a smile and a wink. Fuck, playing with him is so much fun.

The same woman I met once before looks up from behind the desk to see who's walked in. I quickly read her name badge: *Grace*. "Are you okay?" she asks with genuine concern in her voice. "What happened to Tammy is awful. Ben called to say Ethan is bringing you in for a statement, and all I could think about is how you must be feeling. Are you okay? Can I make you a cup of tea, or a coffee?"

Ethan nearly tears the door off the hinges as he enters the station. "I was telling Ethan in the car how safe I felt knowing I was with him and I was coming here." Grace is eating up the quiver and sadness in my voice. I look down and try to force my eyes to well with tears, but I have nothing to cry about. "Poor Tammy," I whisper.

"Ethan, Ben said you can use his office for Anna's statement."

"Could I get a bottle of water please, Grace?"

"Sure." She smiles gently.

"This way." Ethan gestures toward the back of the station. He wraps his hand around my upper arm and squeezes painfully. His touch makes my skin crawl with revulsion, but also with the certain knowledge that he's evil. I just need to find out how he fits into all of this. Once I do, it'll determine how to kill him. If he touches kids, I'd be happy to make it a long, slow, drawn out death. If he likes to beat women, which I've already had a small taste of, then it'll be equally painful. "You're going to tell me everything I want to know," he whispers in my ear as he pulls me toward Ben's office. He closes the door and roughly shoves me in a chair.

"You're so violent, Ethan. Do you have a problem?"

"Who are you and what are you doing here in Bankstown Creek? I'm sick of you not answering me."

"Are you going to hit me again?" I flutter my lashes at him.

He walks around and sits at Ben's desk. I scan the room and see three family photos proudly displayed on Ben's desk. I know this used to be Dad's office, but nothing has changed at all. Even the desk is the same. I sit back and cross my arms in front of my chest, looking to see the leg of the desk that has my initials carved into it. I did it once when I was about ten, and I had to stay home from school because I wasn't feeling well and Dad had to bring me into work. He had to leave for something and I got bored, so I carved AB into the leg. It was my small demonstration of defiance. I glance at the leg and see my initials are still there. "Who are you?"

I flick my eyes up to Ethan but remain stoic. "You'll find out soon enough."

The door creaks open as someone knocks on it. I turn and see Grace walking in holding a bottle of water for me. "Here you go." She places it on the desk and gently pats my shoulder. "Let me know if you need anything," she offers in a gentle voice.

"Thank you," I reply with the same softness. She walks out and I instantly return to my normal self. "Now, are you going to take my report?"

Ethan purses his lips together while his nostrils flare with sheer anger. He turns to the computer and enters his details.

"Is Ethan treating you right?" Ben asks as he walks into his office. The hour I've been in here feels like an eternity. It's been a constant loop of Ethan attempting to get information while I toy with him like a puppet on a string. Although it started out as fun, I'm now bored.

"He's been the perfect gentleman, haven't you, Ethan?" I glance over to him and smile.

Ethan stands and moves toward the door. "Are you taking Anna home?" he asks Ben.

"No, I need my car," I say. Ethan's bitter smile tells me he knows he's been defeated in this instance. I'm at least one step ahead, and we both know it. One day my arrogance might get me into trouble, but until that day happens, I'm not going to stop being me.

Ethan leaves without another word, and I stand to walk over to Ben. "You can stay at my house tonight considering this is your last night here."

"With everything that's happened, I'll add another day or two to my stay." Besides, now I really need to know what Ethan is hiding in Bankstown Creek. I need to find out where it is, and I need to burn it to the ground, or I need to stop it. "You know I can't stay."

"I know," he acknowledges. "Have you got your stuff?"

I tap my jeans pocket to check for my car key. "I do." Ethan still has my phone and I doubt I'll see it back, and even if I do I know he'll have fitted a program to track me.

We walk out and I stop where Grace is. "Thank you for being so kind."

"You're welcome."

Ben wraps his arm around my waist and we continue toward the front door. "Anna!" I hear Ethan calling. "You left your phone behind." He thrusts it into my hands so I have to take it.

"Did I? With everything that happened today, I must've overlooked it." I hold the phone up and smile. "Thank you, Ethan." I slide it into my pocket.

The curiosity is burning through me as Ben drives us back so I can pick up my car. I really want to know what Ethan's done to my phone, but I don't have my computer or even the phone I use for work on me. "Are you sure you don't want to stay with me tonight? You can sleep in the guest room, and I promise I'll keep my hands to myself." He glances at me as he drives. "It even has a lock if you're worried."

He's adorable. "No, I can't. Maybe tomorrow we can have lunch or dinner. But don't you have to work?"

"I'm still on vacation for a few more days. Maybe you'll consider staying until I go back to work?"

I hate this. I really like Ben, but I can't keep putting off the inevitable. I have to kill him, and soon, before I do something stupid like change my mind. "I'm not sure if I can," I honestly reply. We drive the remaining distance to my car in silence. I stare out the window at the traffic. Bankstown Creek has changed in some ways since I left, but not as much as I thought it would have. The thing I notice most is the number of trucks that use the main road as a thoroughfare. Bankstown Creek isn't a large town by anyone's standard. There must've been a bypass or interstate built close to make it easier for the trucks. Ben pulls up beside my car where the front of the restaurant has been taped off. There are a few groups of people clumped out in front whispering and talking about what they think has happened. "Thank you for the ride," I say as I get out of the car.

"Anna, wait." Ben leaps out of the car and jogs over to me. "Come back to my house and we can talk." He reaches out for me.

My shoulders loosen as I shake my head. There's a hard lump in my throat while I recoil from his touch. I look up at him and breathe in deeply. "I can't," my voice breaks. I hold both my hands up as I back away from him. "I can't," I say, mustering as much authority as I can. "I just can't." My stomach churns with worry. I get into my car and take off out of the parking space with my rear wheels spinning and screeching.

I need to get away from him.

I'm braced beneath a veil of dread for what's about to come. "Shit," I say as I remember the stupid phone Ethan handed back to me. I lower my window and toss the phone out into the shrubs and overgrown grass. A truck passes by me hitting speeds that I admire for something so large and heavy. Kudos to truck drivers for the work they do.

I drive another few miles and pull over to check that Ethan hasn't tampered with my car again. On close inspection, I determine that I'm in the clear and head directly for the cabin. Once inside, I go straight to the laptop and open it up to check the perimeter in case there have been any breaches. Thankfully, other than a few animals crossing by the cameras, it appears that no one is aware of where I am.

I close the computer and walk over to the fridge to grab a bottle of water. There's a nagging feeling of things not being right. Too many questions have been left unanswered, but I'm positive the answers will present themselves.

And soon.

Chapter Nine

S ince I've been back here, my sleep has been shit. My brain is constantly churning as I try to figure out this puzzle, even though a lot of the key pieces are still missing. It's still dark out but I can't sleep. I push the covers off my body and head into the living room to get some work done. No use staying in bed when I could be productive.

I open my laptop and pop my earpiece in. Dialing Agent, I have to wait longer than usual for him to answer. "I was just about to call you," he starts.

I furrow my brows and stare at the screen. "At this time of the morning?"

"We have a problem," he says.

The blood in my veins cools with those words. "What is it?"

"Ethan Martelli is an alias."

I fucking knew he wasn't who he said he was. "Who is he?"

"Ethan Martelli was created ten years ago. His real name is Anthony Mancini Jr., also known as Tony."

"The son of the guy paying for the hit on Ben?"

"The same."

"This is all tied in together," I say to myself. "Is there anything else?"

"Ben Pearson's parents weren't killed by a drunk driver."

"Why would he lie to me?"

"Sorry, he didn't. It was made to look like the other driver was drunk, but their deaths were a hit too."

"What?" I scrub my hand over my face trying to piece this all together. "Who ordered that?"

"Anthony Mancini."

"He ordered a hit on Ben's parents, and now Ben?"

"Exactly."

"Why?"

"I have no idea, but I'm still searching. When I find out, I'll let you know."

"By the way, order me a new phone, and make sure it's locked down."

I take the earpiece out and throw it on the table beside my laptop. Sitting back on the sofa, I cross my arms in front of my chest as I think about the various puzzle pieces starting to come together.

"What am I missing?" I unfold my arms and sit forward closer to my laptop. "What aren't I seeing?" My mind is racing back and forth as I try to figure this out. I leap to my feet and head into the kitchen. In one of the drawers I find a notepad and pen. "Okay, this is what I know." I start scribbling things down on the paper. "Ben's parents were killed six years ago." I write that at the top. "Tony Junior became Ethan ten years ago." I swipe the pad and pen off the kitchen counter and beeline it back to my laptop. I dial Agent and put it on speaker. "Get me into the police personnel records again."

"Give me a second. Have you found something?"

"Maybe. I need to double-check something."

Agent taps on his keyboard. "Coming through." A window pops up on my laptop screen with the police department's personnel files.

I search through Ethan's file. "You came to Bankstown Creek nine years ago, a year after you changed your name." I flick back and see there's a detailed record of his other placements in other police departments. "Can you have a look and check its validity of anything before Ethan came to Bankstown Creek?"

"Give me a minute."

"When did you say Tony Mancini's son died?"

"Nearly eleven years ago."

"And he had two sons. One died, and the other disappeared. Obviously, the one who disappeared is Ethan."

"It is."

"Six years ago, Ben's parents were killed in a hit." I switch to Ben's personnel file and look to see where he was six years ago. "And he was in narcotics and special investigations."

What can't I see?

The link is there, but I'm struggling to put it together.

"Before Bankstown Creek, Ethan's record is a complete forgery," Agent confirms.

"Hmmm." I hang up on Agent and stare at the computer. "Fuck," I curse under my breath. I can't kill Ben until I know what I'm up against, because they might come at me from any direction. "Come on, Anna, think." I scrunch my eyes closed and tap on my forehead trying to make sense of everything. "Fuck!" I pick my water bottle up and throw it across the room. Dad would always tell me to calm down and breathe. He'd tell me to calm my mind because once it was at peace, I'd be able to see things that frustration could conceal. "Dad, I need some help," I say aloud.

Closing my eyes, I take several deep breaths as I attempt to relax my mind. So many images are clouding my attempt at peace, they are making it impossible to focus on the problem. It takes me what feels like a lifetime before the squirrels in my head quiet down and I can focus on nothing but my breath. My mind remains quiet before a flash of the interview Ben gave forcefully pushes itself forward.

I open my eyes and sit staring at my laptop. "Wait, did I miss something?" I scoot forward on the sofa and search for that interview.

The moment I find it, I replay it and watch Ben as he clearly states, "Approximately two hours ago the Bankstown Creek Police Department intercepted a truck suspected of carrying illegal firearms. Upon inspection, we discovered the truck actually contained a large amount of cocaine. The street value of these drugs is in the vicinity of eight million dollars. Bankstown Creek PD has been working closely with other law enforcement agencies and even though we had expected a shipment of guns, we're happy to have prevented these drugs from hitting our streets. Thank you very much for your time."

A slow smile tugs at my lips. There it is. To me it's obvious, but there's still a question I need answered, and the only person who can answer it is Ben.

But first, I need to pay my friend Ethan Martelli a visit.

Pulling up in front of the station, I lock my car and head inside. Grace looks up and smiles when she sees me. "Hi, Anna." She crinkles her brows, appearing confused.

"Is Ethan available?"

"I haven't seen him yet this morning. Hang on I'll go check. He may have snuck in here from the entrance in the back." She leaves the counter at the front and walks to the back of the office. Grace returns within a few moments and shakes her head. "He's not here. But I'll give him a call." She picks the phone up and dials his number. "Hi, Ethan." Grace looks over to me and smiles. "Aha." She nods. "No, nothing like that. Anna is here and she's asking for you." The smile on her face slowly drops. "Okay then." She hangs up and looks over at me. "Ethan said he'll be here in a few minutes."

"Thank you, Grace." I turn and walk over to the window to wait for Ethan. I see a police cruiser tear down the street and pull up next to my car. Ethan looks up to see me staring at him. I smile and offer him a condescending little wave. He gets out of the car and aggressively slams the door shut.

He jogs up to the front and walks in with his chin up and a deadly snarl when he sees me. "I wasn't expecting you today," he says with a bite.

He's angry. *Good.* "No one ever expects me..." I pause for a dramatic effect. "Ethan."

His jaw tightens as his eyes widen. "Why don't we head into Ben's office where we can talk?" He grabs me roughly around the top of my arm and pulls me along. Ethan digs his fingers into me as he hurries toward Ben's office. He shoves me into the office before looking down the corridor and closing the door. "You're proving to be a pain in my fucking ass," he spits contemptuously.

"I'm sorry, Tony, that's the last place I want to be a pain. Unless you're into anal, then being a pain in the ass would suit you."

Ethan stands taller while crossing his arms in front of his chest. He straightens to his full height in order to attempt intimidation. I love knowing I've gotten under his skin. "Who's Tony?" his voice croaks, giving him away to me.

"Tony?" I scrunch my forehead and tilt my head to the side. "Did I say Tony?" I walk backward and lean against the wall. "Oops."

"Who are you?" His jaw tightens.

This is so much fun for me. I know who he is, but he has no idea who I am. *Fun times.* "You see, that's why I'm here." I take a breath and smile. I'm so in my element. "Ten years ago you created an alias, and nine years ago you infiltrated Bankstown Creek Police Department." His jaw relaxes as he takes a step backward. "Why here and what has Ben got to do with it?" I make sure to keep my voice eerily calm.

Ethan visibly swallows as he casts his eyes down my body. "Who are you?" He's not going to tell me anything, but my goal was for him to be aware that I know who he is while he has no idea who I am. I can only imagine how sweat is bleeding from his pores or even how fast his heart is hammering in his chest.

"Oh, Tony," I sigh as I push off the wall and walk toward him. I stop in front of him and fix his collar. "There's only going to be one winner in this, and it won't be you." I gently pat his chest. "Tony, Tony, Tony." I lean in and give him a kiss on the cheek before opening the office door and cockily strolling out of the office. Grace does a double take at me as I walk out. "Bye, Grace," I say in a chirpy voice.

"Bye." She returns her attention to the work she's doing as I walk out to my car.

The drive over to Ben's doesn't take me long, and I'm hyperaware of all my surroundings. If I haven't tipped Ethan over the edge yet, it won't take him long before he calls reinforcements, or tries to take matters into his own hands.

I wasn't planning on seeing Ben again, not until I killed him. But I know he's part of why Ethan is here, and I need to figure it all out before this situation spins out of control. Once I'm in his driveway, I get out of the car and look around. My stomach twists with anticipation. I'm on the verge of figuring this out. I just need more time. Though I don't think I have a lot of that left before everything comes crashing down.

I gulp in a deep breath and walk up to his front door. Lifting my hand, I knock several times and wait for Ben to answer. He opens the door and crinkles his brows in shock. "Anna?"

"Hey." I smile and draw back my shoulders. "Can I come in?"

Ben steps aside. "Of course." He closes the door behind me, then leads me into the kitchen. "Are you okay?"

"I am. Um." I glance over to his fancy coffee machine, then back to him.

"Do you want a coffee?"

"Yeah, I do. Thanks."

The tension between us is thick and it coats the air with foreboding suspicion. "Are you sure you're okay?" Ben repeats as he prepares two coffees.

"I need something from you."

He nods once but doesn't say anything until he brings over two coffees. "Ethan called me about ten minutes before you showed up."

Predictable. I lift my coffee and take a sip. "Did he?"

Ben nurses the coffee mug in his hands and slowly nods. "He did." I wait for him to elaborate. "He told me he doesn't trust you." I feel myself smirking. "He told me to be careful of you."

I half shrug as I shake my head. "Do you think I can't be trusted?"

"I don't know what to think of you." He visibly swallows and lowers his eyes as if he's embarrassed by something. "I like you," he whispers. "But you're overly reserved and I'm struggling with that."

"What part?" I ask.

"Both. I don't know how to feel about you." He lifts his chin and looks away. "I mean..." He gulps again and turns to lean his hip against the kitchen counter. "I don't know if it's the danger of not knowing anything about you that I like, or if it's you. Just you."

"You think I'm dangerous?" I don't like him thinking that I'd hurt him. Ironic really, considering I came here to kill him.

He runs his hand through his hair and stares at the counter between us. "I don't know," he responds earnestly. "I'm trying to figure you out."

I lower my coffee as I contemplate my next move. I take my phone out of my pocket and dial Agent. "Are you with the hottie?"

I completely ignore his ridiculous question. "I need a satellite search." Ben's head snaps toward me. His lips slightly part and his forehead crinkles. "I need building and infrared in a hundred-mile radius."

"What am I looking for?"

"Seemingly abandoned buildings that have any kind of activity." Ben pushes off from the counter and takes a step back.

"I'll get it to you as soon as I can."

I hang up and lower my phone, waiting for Ben's questions. "Who are you?" he finally asks.

"My name *is* Anna."

Ben runs his hands through his hair again as he begins to pace back and forth. "What are you?" he repeats. "You're not a corporate headhunter, are you?"

"I promise you I'll tell you who and what I am when the time comes, but I need to ask you a question."

"I knew you were different from the moment I met you, but you know what confirmed it to me?"

"What?" I need to know so I don't make the same mistake again.

"When Tammy was shot." He purses his lips together. "You didn't go into shock. Your reaction lacked trauma."

Shit. "I—"

Ben shakes his head as he lowers his chin and tilts it to the side. He lifts his hand to stop me talking, before taking several deep breaths as he refuses to look at me. "Who are you?" he asks in a smaller, calmer voice.

"Ben, the only thing I ask of you is to trust me."

"How can I trust you when everything about you is a lie? Not only a lie, but one you're refusing to come clean about?"

"Stop being so damned dramatic, Ben."

He slowly turns his head to stare at me. "Dramatic?" His shoulders droop forward with resignation. "I thought we had something." Ben gestures between us. There's a long uncomfortable pause before Ben finally lifts his chin to look at me. "You said you needed something from me, what is it?"

"The drug haul you stopped."

"What about it?" Ben wraps his hands around the coffee mug and lifts it to his mouth.

"Was it a truck carrying the drugs?"

"Yeah, it was."

"What type of truck?" My phone rings and I swoop it off the counter to answer. "What did you find?"

"There are several buildings I've found that are either abandoned or, on closer inspection, are engaged in some activity. However, there's one that stood out to me and I'm confident it's the one you're looking for."

"What is it?"

"It's an old dairy that's ostensibly operational." I crinkle my brows as I wait for Agent to finish. "But here's the thing; there are no cows anywhere near the dairy. Not one."

I hang up and look at Ben. "What type of truck was hauling the drugs?"

"An old milk tanker." My mind reels as the pieces of the puzzle finally start coming together. I jump to my feet and rush out of the room with

Ben only steps behind me. "God damn it, Anna, what just happened?" He grabs my upper arm to stop me.

I swing around and smash my mouth to his. His hand tightens around my upper arm before he loosens his fingers and draws me closer to him. Our bodies push into each other as our passionate kiss deepens. I pull away, breaking our connection. Ben rubs his hands up and down my arms as he lowers his head and leans his forehead against mine. "You deserve the truth," I say. "But for now, I can't give it to you."

"Let me in," he whispers.

A lump forms in the base of my throat. With regret, I step backward to create a distance between us. I hate having feelings for Ben. I should've killed him when I first agreed to the job and not become more personally involved. Wrestling with my head is also clouding my judgement. My brows pull together as I struggle to find the right words. "I need some time. Then I promise, I'll tell you as much as I can."

"Fuck," Ben grumbles as he steps back. "As much as you can? Come on, Anna, give me something...anything." Ben shrugs slowly as he desperately seeks answers. "Please."

"I'll give you what I can, but not yet." I can't stay any longer because I need to sort this out. I open the front door and turn to walk out to my car.

"Anna," Ben calls.

I don't stop to acknowledge Ben. Instead, I get in my car and pull out of the driveway fast enough that he won't be able to follow me. I head back to my cabin so I can put together a game plan for how to deal with Ethan.

CHAPTER TEN

I haven't slept all night. The one thing I've always been able to do is focus and keep my head in the game. Being in the business I'm in, I can't afford to make mistakes.

But Ben...

I shouldn't have become involved with him; what we had should've stayed remained a one-night stand. I hate how I'm questioning myself over Ben. It shouldn't be this difficult.

"Pull yourself together," I whisper as I push the covers off me and sit on the edge of the bed. "You have work to do, so do it." I stare at an invisible spot on the floorboards as I stumble over my own feelings. "You have a job to do," I repeat with more assertion.

But first, I need to sort out Ethan.

Somehow, I have to lure him out here so I can have the quiet to work. Ethan undoubtedly will be searching for me, especially now that he knows I know who he is. Before I get ready for the day, I bring up the surveillance of the cabin and check to make sure he hasn't found me. I'm not a fan of being surprised by an ambush. I head into the kitchen to make a coffee as I review all the footage from last night.

Nothing is suspicious or out of the ordinary, so I can proceed with what I have to do. I finish my coffee and head into my bedroom so I can get ready to end this, once and for all.

"Hey, Grace," I say as I walk into the station. "Is Ethan around?" I glance toward the back to see if he's here.

"He hasn't come in today. He called and said he wasn't feeling well." Not feeling well, my ass. "Do you want me to call him and let him know you're looking for him?"

I tap the counter twice, then turn to walk out. "No, that's okay. I'm sure we'll cross paths," I say as I throw my hand up over my head in a wave. I slide into my car and contemplate calling him, but I know he's out searching for me so it's a matter of me finding him before he finds me.

"Where would you be hiding?" I ask myself as I pull out of the station. Instantly, my mind goes to the first time I met Ethan, and I head straight toward the same spot. If he's half as smart as he thinks he is, he'll be waiting for me.

I pull onto the main road, and travel below the speed limit just waiting for him to follow. I keep checking my surroundings with the anticipation that I'll see the familiar red and blue lights pull in behind me.

It takes no longer than two minutes to see a car pull in behind me. I'm skeptical because it's not the police cruiser but when he drives right up to my bumper and drafts on my back end, I smile knowing Ethan is at least smart enough to bring his own car and not the police cruiser, which would have GPS tracking. I slow my speed and keep a careful eye on Ethan as other cars fly by. It takes Ethan little time to pull back and flash his lights once we're alone. I know what he wants, so I'm careful to pull over down an isolated street.

He parks the car and walks toward the passenger side of mine. *Let the games begin.* Regardless of what happens from here on in, someone will die, and that someone won't be me.

He opens the door to my car and slides in. Ethan's holding a gun that's not police issue. He cautiously looks around to make sure no one sees us. This is going to be tricky, but so much fun too.

"Nice to see you." I smile over at him.

"I know you're not staying in town." He turns to ensure he hasn't been seen. With Ethan being satisfied we're alone, he turns and slams his elbow in my chest causing all the wind to leave my lungs. "To your cabin, 15," he spits as he jabs the gun into my side.

I take a moment to suck in a breath and recalibrate. I wasn't expecting him to figure it out yet. This could potentially be a problem. "You finally figured out who I am." I slam my foot on the accelerator making the car fishtail and slide as I head toward my cabin. He may have the upper hand, but my moment will come and I'll annihilate him.

With a snarky chuckle and eye roll, he sits back in the seat. "The famous 15," he says with a boastful tone. "Here she is, caught by none other than Tony Mancini." He puffs his chest out with pride as he attempts to steal the spotlight from me.

"Do you always refer to yourself in third person when you're being cocky?" He smacks me on the side of the head causing me to jolt the car sideways. "Oh dear," I say with sarcasm. "Did I embarrass the great Tony Mancini?" I laugh off his reckless attempt to intimidate me.

"Shut up," he screams in fury. Spittle flies from his mouth. His chest is heaving as he glares at me. He pulls his phone out his pocket and dials someone. "Dad, I have her," he says with conviction and pride. "I'll send the coordinates once we're there." I try to listen into the conversation, but the volume is low and I can't hear what his father is saying. He turns toward me and grins as he cocks an eyebrow. "I'll pass that on." He ends the call and holds his phone on his lap. "You and I, Anna, are cut from the same cloth." Ethan clicks his tongue to the roof of his mouth. "We could've been unstoppable together."

"Ew," I say with dramatic flair. "No, thanks."

He drops his phone between his legs and turns to punch me in the upper arm. "Why my father hired you, I have no idea. I could've taken Pearson out, because I'm clearly superior to you." He snorts as he casts his eyes over my body. "Fucking top assassin, my ass. Now I know the rumors are only an urban legend, probably manufactured by you so people are intimidated."

I hold in my own laugh because I need to know more about why I was hired. "What exactly do you have planned for Ben?" I turn down the off-road trail that leads to my cabin.

There's a long pause from Ethan as he keeps a wary eye on me and on where we're going. "He wouldn't take the bribe," Ethan starts.

Bribe? "What bribe?" I ask, waiting for him to tell me everything I need to know. With Ethan's bragging, it will be easy to tease out, especially considering he thinks he's superior to me.

He rolls his eyes and snickers. God, I hate those damn condescending smirks. "Dad said he's looking forward to meeting you tomorrow when he arrives. He said he wanted to be here today but he had some *business* to take care of." His upper lip stiffens. I pull up about twenty yards from the entrance of my cabin. Ethan looks around and scoffs. "This is where you live?" He again pokes the gun into my side. "Out."

I open the door and carefully slide out while keeping an eye on Ethan. "Now what?"

"Lead the way, and if you try to run, I'll shoot you in the back."

I love how confident he is. It'll make tearing him down even more fun. "You're holding a Beretta Elite on me. Do you honestly expect me to outrun a bullet?" *No wonder his father hired me to do the job. His son is a moron.*

I walk toward the cabin and use my fingerprint to open the door. "Sit." He scopes the room before spotting one of two chairs over in the dining room. "There." He points with the gun before moving it to be back on me. I walk over and sit on the chair. "Rope."

"No, Anna," I say with a smirk. He slams the side of the gun into my jaw causing my head to jerk to the side. Damn, that hurts, but I'm not afraid of Ethan or his gun. All I need is an opportunity to get to my safe room, but first I need to gather as much intel from Ethan as he can be tricked into giving. Because once I have him where I want him, he'll shut down and won't talk, especially considering he's aware of my ruthless reputation.

"Everyone's a fucking smart-ass," he says. "Where do you keep the rope?"

"Oh, I thought you were calling me Rope, and that's why I said no, my name is Anna."

He slams me once again, this time in my stomach causing me to double over as I try to suck in enough breath to work through the pain. "Fucking comedian. Sit." He grabs me by my shirt and throws me onto the chair. I play into it, not fighting back because essentially, I still have a job to do.

Ethan's problem is that his anger is mixed with cockiness and ego, making him unable to see the situation for what it is. It's also perfect for me, because the more he believes he has the upper hand, the easier it'll be for me to gather all the information I need, then finally end him like he deserves. He rustles around in the drawers in the kitchen and finds a roll of duct tape. He tapes my arms behind my back while leaving my feet free. Once he's secured me, he steps back and smiles. "Where should I start?" Ethan licks his lower lip as he stares at my body. "I really do like you, Anna, and it's a shame it didn't work out between us." He drags the other chair over and sits opposite me. "I think we should have some fun before my father arrives tomorrow." I've seen that evil glint before. Damon looked at me with that same hunger all those years ago when he and Nox kidnapped me and killed my father.

"If you want to have fun, then by all means." My interpretation of fun is very different from his, especially considering how he's looking at me. *Dirty pervert.*

Ethan rocks back in the chair while staring at me. "Pearson is a fucking idiot, isn't he?" I take in a sharp breath and turn away from Ethan. "Look at me!"

I'm crushing his ego by dismissing him. In a painfully slow way I turn and arch a brow. "What?" I shrug as if I'm bored by him.

"I said Pearson is an idiot."

I let out a low grumble. "I heard you. I just don't care what you have to say about him."

Ethan's tongue peeks out as he wets his lower lip. His eyes blaze with fire as he forcefully jumps to his feet, takes a step forward, and backhands me with so much force it nearly knocks my chair over. He grabs my chin and squeezes it between his fingers. "You'll be dead soon, so..." Ethan stares at me before lowering his head and licking my lips.

I remain calm as he assaults me. "Pearson is going to be heartbroken when he finds your broken and used body on the side of the road." Ethan snorts with laughter as he backs away and sits on the chair opposite me. "I might even dump you on his front lawn. What a nice surprise that'll be for the fucker." He shakes his head. "I owe him for killing my brother. I'll deliver you to him, let him mourn, then slit his fucking throat."

Wait, what did Ethan say? Ethan's brother was shot in a gun-related incident. "Ben killed your brother?" I ask, desperate for all the blanks to be filled in. Ethan hacks back a groan from his throat, turns his head, and spits on my floor. "This is my home. Can you not be such a fucking pig?"

Ethan stands and slams his fist into my stomach, winding me again. "Fucking whore," he says as he spits again.

When I kill him, I'm going to do it slowly. And I'll take the utmost pleasure from doing it, too. Ethan sits again and stares at me. "How did Ben kill your brother?"

"You're as good as dead once Dad arrives, so I might as well tell you." He thrusts his chest out with an imitation of superiority. These boys will never learn. "Ben shot my brother nearly eleven years ago when he found him robbing a drug store." A mafia head's son was robbing a drug store? "My brother was a stupid, strung-out junkie, but he didn't deserve to die like that. I made it my mission to make Pearson bleed, one way or another. The perfect opportunity came when we moved out here. It gave me a chance to become a cop and keep them away from my family's drug business, and it also gave me the opportunity to get close to Pearson."

"There's no record of you before you came to Bankstown Creek."

"You've done your research. Good, because I've done my research on you. 'Top assassin in the world' my ass." He uses air quotes, then laughs with malice. "What you are is a joke, *15*," he snidely says my professional name.

I need him to clarify everything before I kill him. "Ben is a revenge assassination? Ben killed your junkie brother, so you're going to kill him?"

Ethan's upper lip lifts in contempt. He stares at me for a moment before finally replying, "The hit was placed on him because he refused to take the bribe."

"Bribe?"

Ethan smiles to himself, then stands and walks over to me. He grips my chin forcefully in his hand and kisses me as he shoves his tongue into my mouth. I should bite it off, but I need to know more about this bribe. He sinks his teeth into my lower lip drawing blood. The metallic taste coats the inside of my mouth and as he pulls back, my blood is on his lips. He licks them slowly and a small smile tugs at his mouth. "I suppose whatever I tell you you're going to take to the grave tomorrow when Dad arrives." He wipes his mouth after he's licked them clean and looks at the back of his hand. "What a shame, you didn't bleed as much as I wanted."

"You have an entire day with me before Daddy arrives," I say, provoking Ethan again.

His snarky look is replaced with anger as he steps forward and slams the back of his hand across my face again. The pain in my cheek explodes, but I hold it together as I lift my head to look at him. "I'm going to have a lot of fun with you, *15*." I hate how he's emphasizing my name, as if it holds no fear for him. "When we moved our drug business to Bankstown Creek one of father's men approached Pearson and offered him money to look the other way."

"But he didn't take it?"

"No, he didn't, and because we're good at what we do, he didn't even know we'd already moved into the area," Ethan boasts. "So, we set up an off-shore account in his name, and deposited money into it every month. If he ever denies it, the money is there in his name." His eyes smile with pride.

"Why do you have several bank accounts then?"

Ethan puffs his chest out and lifts his chin. "I will say this, you're thorough. Pity you're not smart enough to know this was going to happen." Here we go again, a rant about how he's superior to me. If only he knew that all he's doing is prolonging his death while feeding me all the information I need to wrap this entire transaction up. "Those accounts are just for fun. I don't need the money, but I love fucking with the police department. Besides, by the time they've figured out I've been syphoning money to myself, I'll be long gone and Ethan Martelli will be nothing more than a memory."

"Why is it important to keep the drugs here in Bankstown Creek?"

"These people are fucking idiots and we can remain here without detection. With all the businesses my father has, this is by far the most lucrative. Dad owes some people money and the drugs turn over the kind of profit we need to keep the payments up. The whores can only fuck so fast, and most of them end up diseased, and need to be put out of their misery. The guns aren't moving as fast as we need because we don't have the monopoly on that yet. And the people we owe wait for no man. There's no delaying their payments."

"So Ben's just an innocent bystander who killed your junkie brother during a robbery and wouldn't take a bribe?"

Ethan sits back in the seat and starts laughing. "We killed his parents too, but the fucker isn't smart enough to realize that was a warning." He taps the side of his temple several times. "Pearson didn't figure it out." He stops laughing and shrugs.

And there is it. All the information I need. "So what you're telling me is that Ben's in your way, and you need to get rid of him?"

"Which is where you come into it, but as it turns out, you're a hindrance and nothing else. If you had put a bullet in his head the way you were supposed to, you'd be richer, he'd be dead, and we'd have free reign in Bankstown Creek."

So Ben's the only thing stopping them from clearing their debt, which is why they need him dead. And they couldn't let just anyone kill him, they need the best, so they hired me. I look down and smile to myself. "Wow," I whisper. This has turned into a clusterfuck.

"What?"

"I could've worked this job easily, but you know what I did?"

Ethan's brows draw in together with concern. "What?"

"I became involved with the hit." I shake my head.

"Sucks to be you, 15. Not only did you not kill the target, but you're gonna die because of it." He takes in a sharp breath as he casts his evil eyes over my body. "I'm going to have a lot of fun killing you. Do you know what I think I might do?"

"Do tell."

"I might even live stream it. Now, how much fun would that be?"

What an idiot. "Sure. Sounds like a blast." *Let's put proof of murder on the Internet and you are so delusional that you think you're above ramifications, that no one will ever come for you. Moron.*

"I'll be known as the man who took down 15." Yep, and you'll put a target on your back forever, because there's always someone who wants the recognition of being the best. That's the difference between me and them; I couldn't care less about the credit whereas most of them need everyone to know who they are. "You know." Ethan stands and saunters over toward me. "You look sexy as fuck sitting there with the bruises I've given you coming up under your skin." He rubs the back of his hand across my throbbing cheek before lifting it over his head and slamming it into my face in an open-handed slap. "Jesus, you have no idea how hot this is." He thrusts his hips forward trying to show me his hard-on.

"Ooph." I clench my jaw together as I narrow my eyes. "You sure you have a dick, Ethan?" I need him to keep hitting me, because the more his focus is on his anger, the less he'll notice me trying to wriggle out of the tape around my wrists.

He slams me again, but this time with so much force that my chair actually tips over to the side. A piercing pain shoots up my arm as I land on it, but I can't give up now, I need him to hit me a few more times to be able to get out of the tape. He picks the chair up and paces back and forth in front of me. "Fuck, you look hot. Not such a big shot now, are you, bitch?"

Bitch...ugh. I hate that word being used when referring to women. It's insulting and degrading. I smile as I lower my chin but lift my eyes. "I'm going to have so much fun with you, Ethan."

He yanks me up out of the chair, grabs my t-shirt around the collar, and slams his fist into my face. I hear the crack of my nose as I go flying backward. But the most important thing is that my hands are now looser from the duct tape. Ethan's in his own little universe where he is the emperor as he stalks toward me, giving me the opportunity to wiggle my wrists free from the tape. His hand darts out and grabs me by the hair as he drags me up. "You're making me so fucking hard. I think it's time you discover what a real man feels like."

He shoots his hand out to smack me again, and this is where Ethan's life is about to change. I block his punch, step forward, and headbutt him square on the nose. In complete shock, he drops his gun and cups his bloody nose and stumbles backward. I quickly grab the now-broken and toppled chair and swing it at Ethan, making him step back further. I drop the chair and punch him on the temple, causing him to collapse to the ground in a heap. I lay a few kicks into his side to make sure he stays down.

I've managed to knock Ethan out. I stare at his beaten body and fight the urge to slit his throat before he wakes from unconsciousness. I lean against the wall and bend at the waist to catch my erratic breath.

My face hurts and my heart hammers inside my chest. I lift my shaky hands to see the tape has cut into the skin around my wrists. "Get it together." I close my eyes and take several deep breaths, calming my frantic mind so I can clearly see what I have to do.

It takes me no longer than a few moments to gather my thoughts and become the professional I am. I open my eyes and get to work while Ethan is still passed out on the floor. I open the safe room, take out rope and zip ties. I make sure to move fast because he'll wake up soon. When he does, I want him to know I've always been in control and he never stood a chance against me. I fasten his wrists together with a zip tie before grabbing him under the arms and dragging his sorry ass into my bathroom. Once in there, I hog-tie his hands together to his feet. I need him completely incapacitated. I don't want him able to move at all. I close the lid to the toilet and sit on it staring at him.

The fucker touched me, and now I feel dirty with his filth. I strip off and jump in the shower to wash off all of Ethan's scum. Closing my eyes, I stand under the stream of hot water. When the water touches my sore and beaten body, it causes me to flinch in pain.

I lower my head and close my eyes as I stretch out my arms to lean against the wall.

"Untie me, you fucking bitch," Ethan grumbles. I turn to stare at him. "Untie me," he says with more force. I shake my head before lowering my chin again to enjoy the heat of the shower. "I'm going to fucking kill you."

I let out a sigh as I focus on the tile in front of me. "You can't be serious."

"Untie me so I can kill you, you fucking cunt."

I laugh at him and take my time washing myself, rinsing the grime of Ethan off of me. He's tied up on the bathroom floor, unable to move. There's nothing sharp he can break to use as a knife, there's nothing in here he can use to harm me. I don't even have a shower door, so he can't break it. I turn off the water and step out of the shower, naked and wet in front of Ethan. His eyes defy his bravado. "Typical idiot." I give him a full view of my naked body before reaching for a towel and wrapping it around me. "I'm going to kill you, Ethan. Slowly and painfully."

"Yeah?" his tone escalates as he clenches his jaw. "Untie me and let's see how far you'll get. Let's make it a fair fight, and I'll fucking kill you."

"A fair fight? Like you beating me with my hands duct-taped behind my back?" A small snort escapes me. "Sure, we can make it fair." I step closer, grab his head between my hands and slam it on the tiled wall behind him. The towel unwraps itself and falls to the floor. "Fair enough?" I ask once the tile cracks from the sheer force of me smashing his head on it.

Ethan blinks rapidly. I step back in time to miss him spitting at me. "You're fucking dead, you hear me, fucking dead."

"I've been doing this a long time, and you're going to have the privilege of being my guest of honor." I reach for my towel and run it through my hair while standing naked in front of him. "You'll pass out at some stage, but rest assured, I'm going to have so much fun hurting you." I walk out of the bathroom to leave Ethan to his own miserable thoughts. At some point, he's going to go into panic mode because he'll realize that nothing is going to get him out of the situation.

"Get back here!"

I finish drying and change into clothes I can work in. I find my earpiece and phone. "Are you okay?" Agent asks when we're connected.

"I've been worse," I reply.

"Do you need Doctor?"

"Don't be ridiculous. What I need is for you to see if there's been another hit put on the cop." I hear his fingers tapping on the keyboard. I look toward the bathroom and take in a breath. "Have Cleaner and Doctor on standby." I hang up on Agent and back up until my legs find my bed.

"Untie me, you fucking bitch!" Ethan's screaming and yelling is doing my head in. He's not shutting up.

I stand and walk to my safe room where I grab one of my handguns and head back into the bathroom. "Is there another target on Ben?"

Ethan spits at my feet again. I lift the gun and shoot his right knee out. "Fuck! You shot me," he screams.

"Is there another hit on Ben?" I repeat.

"I don't know," he shouts as he writhes in pain.

I move my aim beside his head and shoot past his ear. Enough to cause that god-awful ringing to last him for a few hours. I leave the bathroom and close the door to muffle Ethan's crying and pleas for help. I pick the phone up and dial Ben. "Hello?"

"Ben."

"Anna, where are you?"

"I need you to do something for me."

"What is it? What's going on? You sound worried."

"I need you not to go anywhere until I get to your house."

"What?"

"Don't go anywhere until I can get to you."

"Why? What's wrong? Are you okay? Do you need help? Where are you?"

"Ben, I'm asking you to stay there. I'll come to you, but please promise me you won't go anywhere."

"Anna—"

"Listen," I cut him off. "I promise I'll explain everything, but I need you to stay until I can reach you. I shouldn't be long." It takes Ben a moment to finally agree. I hang up, leave the phone on the kitchen counter, and take a steak knife out of the drawer. Opening the door to the bathroom, I find Ethan desperately attempting to escape from the ropes binding his feet and wrists.

I kneel beside him and take off his shoes and socks. "What are you doing?" he asks.

"I'm working." I hold the knife to the sole of his foot, stab it in and drag it up. "This way, even if you do manage to get out of the restraints, I know you're not going to get very far."

Ethan's blood curdling screams are music to my ears. "Stop! Stop!" he pleads.

"You prefer to use your fists so you can show how macho you are." I smile at him as I stab his other foot and slit it open. "I prefer to make you bleed." I stand and look down at my knife skills. "I'll be back. Don't go anywhere." I wink at Ethan as I close the bathroom door and head into the kitchen. I call Agent once again. "Keep an eye on him."

"I will."

I grab my car keys and make my way out so I can go to Ben.

CHAPTER ELEVEN

"What the fuck happened to your face?" Ben asks when he opens the door and sees me standing with a hood over my head. He reaches out and lifts my chin to look at him. "Who did this?" His brows draw in together and his chest expands. "Where can I find him?"

"Ben, I need you to calm down. Besides, I've taken care of who did this to me." I point to my face.

"Who is he and where is he?" Ben backs away from his door and disappears up the stairs. When he returns he's checking the ammunition in his gun. He stops when he sees me. His jaw is tight and his shoulders are high and rigid. "Where the fuck is he?"

I step closer and place my hand on his chest. "You have to trust me when I say I'm taking care of it." I lower my hood and clear my throat. I rub my fingertips over my tender lips as I gather the words I need. "I need to take you back to my house."

"Why?"

"Because you're not safe here."

His forehead scrunches. "What do you mean?"

"I've given you no reason not to trust me, and now I need you to do exactly that."

"Anna—"

"Please," I say, stopping him from saying anything else. "Come with me."

I reach my hand out to take his. Ben hesitates for only a few heartbeats before looking down to take my hand. "Your wrist." With his gun firmly tucked into his jeans, he grabs both of my hands and looks down at the abrasions from the duct tape. "What the fuck happened?" He drops my hands and slowly raises his to sweep some loose hair off of my face. "I'll come with you," he finally says.

"Thank you. But we need to leave right now." I step back toward the door. "I mean, *right* now."

Ben frowns but shuffles closer toward me. "Tell me you're safe, Anna."

"I'm safe." *But you're not.* "I need you to come with me now."

"I'm coming."

"And I also need you to not ask questions until we get back to my cabin."

"Your cabin?" I silently plead with him not to ask anything. "Okay," he acknowledges.

I drive well above the speed limit to get back to the cabin. I pull up in front and turn the car off. Staring at the wheel, I take in a deep breath. "When we get inside, I need you to not react."

"What does that mean?"

"I need you to let me explain before you say anything. But I also have to tell you not to try to take me down, because I don't want to hurt you."

"What?" his elevated voice and puzzled stare both tell me how confused he is. I lean under my seat and take out one of my Glocks. Ben's eyes widen, then narrow before he looks down at his lap. "What's happening?"

I open the door and slide out. "I need you to follow me inside."

It takes Ben a few seconds before he hesitantly eases out of the car and stands beside the door. "This is where you live?"

"It's my cabin, Ben. I've owned it for years."

He looks around, delaying his response. "You have?"

"We need to get inside." Wary and hyper-alert, I turn to make sure my unwelcome guests haven't arrived yet. I walk up to the front door and use my fingerprint to unlock it.

Ben pauses before entering behind me. I close and lock the door behind him, where he stands and looks around the room. Everything happened so fast that I haven't even had a chance to assess the chaos. One chair is broken and the other is lying on its side. There are a few small puddles of blood on the floor and the sofa has been turned over. "This is a crime scene."

"It is," I confirm.

"You were attacked here?"

"I was."

"And the perpetrator?"

Torment simmers deep in my chest as I stand beside Ben, knowing I'm going to have to tell him everything if I want to keep him safe. I don't even recall the moment I decided I wasn't going to kill him. "There's something I have to tell you," I start.

"At this point I think there's a lot you need to explain. Like, why..." he pauses and runs his hand through his hair. Ethan releases a muffled groan of pain and Ben shoots over toward my bedroom. "Who is that?"

I run ahead of him and stand in front of the door, blocking his entrance. "Before you go in there, I have to explain something." He reaches for his gun, and I shake my head. "Don't do that," I warn. His hand inches closer to his waistband in defiance. "Fuck!" I yell as I reach and grab my gun before he has a chance to get to his. With my gun pointed on him, I indicate for him to throw his on the sofa. "I don't want to do this, Ben."

Silently, he tosses it over to the sofa and lifts his hands in surrender. "What happened?"

"Put your hands down." I lower my gun, leaving it resting against my thigh. Ben eyes his gun and I groan. "Please, don't make me shoot you," I beg.

"Who are you?" he finally asks.

"My name isn't Anna Moore. My real name is Anna Brookes. Daughter of Harry Brookes."

There's a small hesitation from Ben. "Police Chief Harry Brookes from Bankstown Creek?" I nod my confirmation. An array of emotions passes over Ben's face. "But you died."

I slowly lift my shoulders. "Clearly not."

Ben steps backward until he's up against the wall. "What's happening?"

"There are some other things you need to know."

"What happened to you? You were presumed dead even though they didn't find your body."

"A lot happened to me, Ben. But you've probably heard of me with a different name."

Ben's entire face hardens while he shakes his head. "What name would I know you by?" he asks as he runs his hand through his hair. "Are you really a headhunter?"

"Technically, I am."

"Technically?" he repeats slowly. "What do you mean by technically?"

I lower my chin to avoid eye contact. I'm not embarrassed by my profession, but I know Ben's going to explode with a bad reaction once I tell him who I am. I brace myself as I prepare to tell him. Worrying my bottom lip between my teeth, I finally raise my chin and pull my shoulders back. "My professional name is 15." Ben holds an intense, cold stare. It takes him a few seconds to register what I've said. The muscles in his neck strain and his nostrils flare. He looks over to his gun and back to me. I lift my gun higher and point it at his chest. "You're not fast enough," I warn. "And I don't want to hurt you."

"15 is a myth. An urban legend, something people have made up."

"*I'm* 15," I repeat.

"No, no you're not." Ben continues to shake his head like he's trying to dislodge my words. "You can't be." I lower my weapon and step back, giving him the chance to go for his weapon. "Why are you saying that?"

"I'm an assassin, Ben."

He steps toward me and grabs my upper arms. "Stop lying, Anna, stop!" His fingers dig into me as he shakes me. "Why are you lying?"

"You know who I am."

Ben's fingers slowly unhitch and he drops his hands to beside him as he steps away from me. He visibly swallows and sucks in several breaths. "Why are you here?" We're interrupted by another small cry from Ethan. Ben and I both look over toward my bedroom. "Who is that, Anna?"

"I'll tell you everything you need to know, but first I need to check on Ethan."

"Ethan? What have you done to him?" I turn my back on Ben and walk into my room. I hear his feet scuffle forward before he calls, "Anna."

I know he has his gun and is pointing it at me. "If you have to shoot me, do it," I say without looking back. A small part of me nags that I shouldn't have turned my back on Ben, but I highly doubt he'll hurt me.

I hear a low grumble following me into the bedroom. I look over my shoulder to see Ben still has his weapon in his hand. I open the door to the bathroom to find Ethan lying on the floor. His leg has a hole from where I've shot him and there's a pool of blood around his feet. "Oh my God, what have you done?" Ben moves forward toward Ethan, but I hold my arm out to stop him.

"Trust me," I say as I look at him.

Ethan opens his eyes and focuses on Ben. "Ben, help me, she's gone insane," he pleads.

"I have to help him," Ben says.

"No, you don't." I step further into the bathroom, lift my leg and place my foot on his open wound. I apply pressure on it, causing Ethan to shriek in pain. "Has anyone else been hired, Ethan?"

"Fuck you, you bitch!" he spits toward me.

I shoot him in the thigh. "Fuck," Ben grumbles but doesn't move to stop me.

Ethan erupts into tears. "Please, please, stop."

"I asked you a question, Tony."

"Tony?" Ben asks in confusion.

"Has anyone else been hired?" I step to the other side, and place my foot on his thigh. Ethan's wails are reminiscent of an animal in agony. I step backward and squat down beside him. "I can make the pain go away, if you tell me what I need to know."

Ethan's eyes are puffy as the tears stream down his face. "I'll fucking die before I give you anything, you fucking bitch." Blood is now mixed with his spit.

I grab a fistful of his hair tilting his head to the side. I lift the gun and place it under his chin. "If I shoot you this way, there's no guarantee it'll travel through your skull and kill you instantly. You could be laying here without enough control of your body to even squirm in pain. I'll move the gun half and inch out causing you so much pain that you'll pray to die, and I'll leave you until your organs shut down from blood loss and finally stop. That could be a day, or a week, or even longer," I say. "Or you could tell me if anyone else was hired, and I could kill you quickly." Ethan's breathing is fast and erratic. He has a few hours at best, but either way, I'm going to get the information I need. "My associate will be calling me with the answer soon, and if you haven't given it to me, I'm going to pump you up with adrenaline and leave you to bleed out tied up in my bathroom. I might even set the cabin on fire while you're in here," I say in a cold unrelenting voice. "Just so I can hear you scream."

"Jesus," Ben murmurs. I look up to him to see his hands trembling slightly.

"Do you want a quick death, Tony? Or do you want me to make you hurt even more than you already do?"

"Q-q-quick," he stutters as he cries heavier.

"Tell me what I need to know." I cock my gun in warning. Ethan lowers his head and slightly nods. "I need you to say it."

"Someone else has been hired," he weeps.

I stand and step backward. "Thank you."

"You're going to help him, aren't you?"

"You'd best leave," I say to Ben.

"Wait, you're not going to kill him, are you?"

"He's as good as dead. I'm a woman of my word. I told him I'll kill him quickly if he tells me what I need to know."

"You can't be serious." I lift my gun, don't even turn to Ethan when I shoot him between the eyes. "What the fuck! Put your hands up, you're under arrest," Ben yells as he points his gun to me.

I can see it in his eyes, he's grappling with what he needs to do. I waltz past Ben into the kitchen. I take two bottles of water out of the fridge and place his on the table. He follows me out, with his gun still drawn. "We need to talk." I push the bottle closer to him.

"I think this actually calls for something stronger than water, don't you?"

"No. You need to remain clearheaded when I tell you what's happening." I open the lid of the water and take a swig.

Finally, Ben lowers his weapon and tucks it into his waistband. "Did you sleep with me to get to Ethan?"

"No. Nothing like that." I lean against the kitchen counter as I glance around the upheaval in my family room. "I didn't know who you were when we first met." He hesitantly reaches for the water. "I was celebrating because I finally killed the man who sent his hitmen to kill my father and kidnap me." Ben's hand stills as he lifts the bottle. "When I was younger, I had a natural talent with hitting the bull's-eye. Dad taught me how to shoot, and how to handle a gun properly. He'd take me to the range so I could practice, and I was cocky." I smile slightly as I relive a difficult time in my life. "I developed a reputation for being precise and also being able to shoot two guns at the same time with extreme precision. Word got out about me, and a man by the name of Ronan Murphy sent his men to take me, and kill Dad."

"Ronan Murphy?" I nod as I glance down at my water bottle. "He trained you?"

"I killed his goons when I was fifteen. They left a gun under the seat of their car and I killed them with it. They were my first kills."

"You were fifteen," his voice warbles with stress. "You killed two people at such a young age?"

"It was either kill, or let them take me away, where they'd break me. Ultimately I was supposed to become Ronan Murphy's personal hitman." I shake my head.

Ben places the bottle on the counter and rubs his hands down his pants nervously. "You were just a kid."

"And now I'm a woman who gets paid very handsomely to kill people."

A small bead of sweat runs down Ben's temple. He tilts his head to the side, then looks over his shoulder toward my bedroom. "Ethan."

"He's not my hit."

"Then who?" I remain quiet, letting him think about his words. Ben's jaw tightens, then loosens as his mouth gapes open with realization. "Me."

"You."

Ben quickly straightens and pulls his shoulders back. "You've been hired to kill me," he says rhetorically. I nod once. "Do you want to kill me?" Not exactly what I thought he'd ask. I shake my head once. "Are you going to kill me?"

I swallow my ragged breath. There's a deep pain in my chest as I purse my lips together. "There was no doubt in my mind that I was going to kill you and make it look like an accident. It was going to be quick and painless, but..."

"But what?"

"Ethan."

"I still don't know what he has to do with this. You called him Tony. Who's Tony?"

"Ethan Martelli is an alias."

"An alias?

"Ethan's real name is Tony Mancini Jr."

Ben turns to gather his thoughts and paces slowly back and forth. He stops and pinches the bridge of his nose. "As in Anthony Mancini the mob boss?" I nod and let it sink in for a moment. "What?" Bewildered, his posture loosens. "What?"

"I was hired by Anthony Mancini to kill you."

Ben grumbles as he stares at me. "What?" he repeats in the same per-plexed tone.

"You stand in the way of the drugs they're processing here and moving out of Bankstown Creek. You didn't take a bribe that was offered to you years ago, and it was also personal to them."

"What?" Ben's stuck in a loop of an unbelievable alternate universe he had no idea was existing right under his nose.

"You killed Ethan's brother in a drug store robbery."

Ben's eyes widen. "Wow," he whispers. "So, this is because I killed his brother *and* some kind of drug operation?"

"Yeah." I stay watching him because there's one more thing I have to tell him. "Ben, you also have to know something else."

"What?"

"They killed your parents."

"No, that was an accident," he counters with conviction.

"It was supposed to be a warning to you. They killed your parents. Tony admitted it to me." I worry my lip between my teeth as I closely watch Ben.

Ben steps forward and leans his arms on the counter. He lowers his chin and takes several deep breaths. "They were killed in a car accident," he says in a small voice.

"The Mancini family had your parents killed as a warning to you because you wouldn't take a bribe."

Silence blankets the room, and a cold chill falls over us. Ben's struggling to process everything, and I'm waiting for him to lose his shit. He sucks in another deep breath as he stares down at the floor. *Shit.* A small crying tremor escapes from his mouth. "I killed my parents." Ben's shoulders slump forward as he pushes off the counter and stands, then stoops over to half his height. He clutches at his chest as he walks over to the sofa, rights it, and collapses onto it.

I don't do feelings. I'm cold and emotionless. *It's who I am.* But in this moment, I feel Ben's pain as he quietly weeps over the murder of his parents. I'm conflicted on what action to take, but this isn't about me. It's about what Ben is feeling. I place my own bottle on the counter and walk over to him. I lay my hand on his shoulder and gently squeeze. "I'm sorry,"

I finally say. "But this is on Mancini, not you." I lift my hand and, sitting down beside Ben, wrap my arm around his shoulders. My body becomes rigid when Ben surrenders and engulfs me in a hug.

"I wish I had known, because I would've killed Ethan...Tony myself."

There's no doubt in my mind Ben would've killed him. My phone rings and I let Ben go so I can answer it. "Agent."

"We have a problem."

"What is it?" I stand and walk away from Ben while keeping my eyes firmly on him.

"There's another target on your hit, and I've been able to find they've been hired from Hunter Inc. by Mancini. There's also something else you need to know."

"What?" I exhale and lean against the wall.

"The bounty on you still stands."

Which means Simon from Cablevision was sent to kill me. It also clarified that Hunter Inc. is still operational even though I killed Ronan Murphy, so that means someone else is running it.

"Get Cleaner and Doctor on standby and wait for further instructions."

"I'll have them en route within minutes."

I hang up and slide my phone back into my jeans. Both Cleaner and Doctor will need to fly in from their respective homes, but by the time they get here, I will have dealt with the Mancinis. I look to Ben and worry my lip between my teeth. "There's a hiccup, Ben."

"What's coming?" he asks with an eerily composed tone.

"Anthony Mancini will be here soon to take us out. Ethan gave him the coordinates of my cabin before I killed him. He won't come alone. He'll bring an army of disposable henchmen and heavy firepower, which means we're both in danger. Also, there's a target on my back because of the hit on Ronan. You remember Simon?"

Ben narrows his eyes and slowly lifts one shoulder. "Simon?"

"Simon from Cablevision? The guy you killed at Mamma's?"

"Yeah."

"That hit was likely meant for me." Ben's brows lift. "You can take my car and leave, but I can't protect you if you do. Without me, you'll likely be dead by morning, if you stay with me, you'll have to hang up your badge and fight dirty, because it's the only way you'll survive."

"I'm not—"

"I can't guarantee your safety either way. But your chances of survival with me are higher than if you try to do this on your own. I've been doing this for thirteen years, and no one's killed me yet." I walk over to him and place my hand on his shoulder. "I'm sorry, but I need you to make your decision now because I need to plan out what I'm going to do." I lift my hand from his shoulder and step back to sit on the coffee table opposite him. "You need to know that either way there's a heavy chance of one or both of us dying. But I'm not going to go down without a fight. Not against that fucker Mancini."

Ben sits forward to lean his elbows on his knees. He drops his head into his hands to cover his face. I know this goes against his ethics as a police officer. "I could call in reinforcements and get help from the department."

"You could," I reply. "And if you do, I have to leave, because you and I both know, it won't work in my favor." I gesture toward the bathroom where Ethan is. "And if your people don't kill Mancini and only lock him up, then the target tightens on you and your sisters."

Ben's shoulders tighten as he straightens. "No one touches my family." He visibly swallows as his nostrils flare. "I'll do whatever you need me to do." His body stiffens as his face becomes cold with hatred.

"I have work to do." A killer will emerge from Ben Pearson. "But for now, we both need to eat and to sleep because tomorrow, your life will change."

CHAPTER TWELVE

The night was restless. Neither Ben nor I slept more than a handful of hours between us. Ben refused to sleep in the bed with me, instead opting for the sofa. I could hear him pacing back and forth throughout the night, while I tossed and turned with my mind working in overdrive.

As light takes over from the darkness, I know I need to push on with today. I may not have slept, but I doubt Anthony Mancini will give me a pass because I'm tired. I sit on the side of the bed and run my hands over my face and through my hair. I grab the hair tie I tucked under my pillow and tie my hair back in a ponytail before heading out to find Ben already up and drinking a coffee. "You didn't sleep either, right?" Ben asks when he sees me. "I've made you a coffee."

"Thank you." I walk over and lift the mug to my lips. "Are you ready?" I ask before taking a sip.

Ben walks around the counter and sits on the barstool beside me. "I have questions."

"I'd be surprised if you didn't."

"You didn't know who I was the night we..."

"Fucked?" Ben nods slowly. "Like I told you yesterday, I had no idea who you were."

"It was merely a coincidence?"

"You were relief to my itch. I was celebrating taking out Ronan Murphy and my twenty-eighth birthday by picking you up and fucking you."

"And then you were hired to kill me?"

"I was."

"What's changed?"

"I'm going to be truthful with you." I take a breath as I stare at him. His eyes are heavy with scrutiny as he hangs on my words. "I don't know," I admit. Ben grits his teeth and lowers his head to focus on his coffee. "The time we've spent together has done something to me."

"What?" he asks without looking at me.

"I feel protective of you. I care about you." Jesus, what the fuck is wrong with me? I sound like a lovestruck teenager. This is ridiculous. Forming a close connection with someone is dangerous not only to me but to them too. "I need your gun," I say as I change the trajectory of this insane conversation.

"What happened between you and Ethan?" I know what he's asking. "Did he..."

"No, he didn't get a chance, though that's where it was headed." I swallow back the mush I'm turning into and stand. "I need your gun," I say again while I hold my hand out to him.

He looks over to the sofa. "It's over there."

I walk over and grab it before returning next to him. I take the clip out and check the gun. "You can't use this today."

"I know."

I walk over to the weapons room and enter the code. Opening it, I walk in and place the police-issue gun on the lip that goes around three of the walls below the shelves that hold all my weapons. I start assembling what we're going to need for today. "Holy shit," Ben says.

"I know."

"This is an armory, Anna."

"I know." I stack the weapons and the ammunition on the small table in the center of the room. I open the long drawer that holds one of my disassembled sniper rifles. I take it out one piece at a time.

"Is that a sniper rifle?"

"Yes." I continue to take pieces out and line them up on the table.

"What's your range? Five hundred yards?"

I cock a brow as I slowly turn to look at him. "Five hundred yards?" I snort with a dismissive chuckle. "If I was an amateur."

"A thousand yards?"

"A thousand yards? I can do that with one hand tied behind my back and a patch over an eye." Ben's brows knit together. "Are you seriously insulting me now?"

"What is it? A mile?"

I stop assembling my sniper rifle and look at him. I flick my hand dismissively. "Is it because I'm a woman that you're guessing such low distances? If I was a man, would it make a difference to you?" Ben takes a small step backward and tilts his head to the side in question. "Wow, and the patriarchy apparently isn't real," I say as I continue with the assembly.

"Come on, tell me. The record stands at nearly four thousand yards."

"That's a cute little number, isn't it?" I condescendingly ask.

"I said nearly four thousand yards. Are you telling me you can accurately shoot over four thousand yards?"

I stop again and take a breath. "Without breaking a sweat," I reply coldly before returning to my weapon.

Ben remains quiet for a few moments as he watches me finish with the sniper rifle. "Do you know what I'm thinking?"

"I'm not a mind reader."

"You're scary as fuck."

I stop and turn to him. "Yes, I am," I confirm. I check the magazines of the other guns and hand him two automatics. "Do you know how to use these?"

"I do."

"Anthony Mancini is due here soon. We're leaving the cabin and going up the mountain, because that will give me the high ground and I'll be able to see what's coming at us. I'll have eyes on Mancini and I'll take him out, but you're going to have to take out everything else that comes our way. I'll also have eyes in the sky to help too. But you need to understand one thing."

"Eyes in the sky?" He looks out the window and up.

I snap my fingers at him. "Pay attention, Ben, because this is life or death."

"I'm listening."

"If Mancini gains the upper hand and gets to me, you *do not* come to rescue me."

"But..."

"There are no buts. This is for your safety. You don't come after me, you let them take me."

"I can't do that."

I take one of my guns and place it to his head. "If you don't give me your word, then we're both as good as dead. And if that's the case, you're done."

"Anna..."

I pull the safety back and let my finger hover over the trigger. "No." I shake my head. "You'll take them and their operation down."

"You're prepared to die for me?"

"I'm prepared to end this," my tone is crisp and clear. I mean every word I speak.

Ben grapples with my request, but finally he nods. "I won't come after you."

I lower my gun, click on the safety, and pack the weapons into my duffel bag and double-check that I have enough ammunition for all of them. After I grab half a dozen bottles of water, I put my earpiece in and press the button to dial Agent. "I need the drones."

"They're about twenty minutes from you."

"We need to move," I say to Ben. "Stay close." I quickly tie my hair back into a severe, tight bun before I sling my sniper rifle over my shoulder. Ben takes the duffel bag and follows me out of the house. "Quiet and quick," I say to him over my shoulder. "We've got a twenty-minute head start," I say to Ben.

"Drones have been deployed," Agent says.

I turn to look at Ben. "You need to hustle," I say as I lead the way. "You need to be on high alert and quiet for me to work. If you see something, or sense something, I need you to tap me anywhere on my body once and motion to where you think the danger is coming from. But, like I said, I have eyes in the sky and Agent will tell me if there's anything I need to know."

"I understand," Ben replies instantly, though simultaneously lifting his chin to look up.

We get to my perfect attack zone and I set up my sniper rifle. I know this rifle like the back of my hand and considering it was over ninety percent assembled before we left the house, it doesn't take me long to finish putting the rifle together. I lie on the ground and look through the scope toward my cabin. "From here on in, I need quiet," I say to Ben.

He kneels beside me as he keeps a focused eye on our surroundings. I watch through the scope, waiting for them to come into view. "Five minutes," Agent says through my earpiece.

I turn to Ben and tap his thigh. "Five minutes."

His shoulders straighten and his jaw tenses. Ben gives me a small, affirmative nod.

A sparkle catches my eye as the whoosh of a bullet misses me by about ten feet. I smirk as I look through my scope and tilt my rifle to find a sniper setting the gauge on his scope. I take in a deep breath to calm my body. The sniper is maybe nine hundred yards down and to the left of where we are. He's partially veiled behind shrubs though I can easily see him.

I hold my finger steady on the trigger as I adjust my scope. He has to wonder if he's about to die, but I bet he's hoping that he'll get one more round off to take me out before he does. It takes me only a few seconds to find the perfect timing for the other sniper to die. I depress the trigger and hear the beautiful sound of the bullet scraping its way out of the chamber. I watch and wait. My heartbeat intensifies while my stomach whirls with anticipation. In my bones I know I've got him, but there's always that miniscule chance I've missed. That hasn't happened in a long time, though.

The bullet lands exactly where I want it to. The sniper's head is blown off his shoulders, exploding with thunderous satisfaction. I take only a second to claim my victory before I move the rifle to see where Mancini is. Ben taps my back once and I turn to see what he has to say. He holds up one hand with all five fingers extended. He points due north, then north-west. It appears Mancini has come prepared. Of course, he's underestimated me, which means this is going to be extra fun for me. He must think Ethan still has the upper hand, and that I'm on my death bed.

I look through the scope again to see two black SUVs pull up in front of my cabin. Four men get out of the first SUV holding assault rifles. They're rigid and on guard, looking around, alert in case something happens. One walks to the other SUV and opens the back door. Another guy gets out and cautiously looks around before indicating for Mancini to get out. Damn it, I don't have a clear shot. He's being blocked by two of his men.

What I need to do is destroy the SUVs so they can't get away.

"You have five on foot coming at you, they're about four hundred yards north. No other vehicles than the two SUVs," Agent says, giving me the details.

"Can you see how many are in the rear SUV?"

"Including Mancini, there's a total of six men in the SUVs and five on the ground."

"How did the five on the ground get here?"

"Motorcycles they're concealed about a mile and a half south."

"Take the motorcycles out."

"I'll send the drones over there now."

I keep watching through my scope as they hover for a moment. Mancini brings his phone to his ear giving me the perfect time to remind him that he's not in charge at all. First things first though. I destroy the engine of the first SUV. Mancini ducks his head down and leaps into the back of the second SUV to protect himself. The driver starts backing that SUV away, but a bullet into that engine means I've completely disabled their mode of transportation.

Mancini stays locked in his car, but I'll get to him. I just need to take his entire entourage down before I can show him my handiwork with his pathetic son. The men all stand still for a moment, then scatter off in different directions. Only two stay on Mancini. Even the drivers are out with their weapons drawn. "You have two coming at you. East and South," Agent says. "Eighty yards."

I have a few seconds before they make it up the hill to take us out. I keep looking through my scope waiting for Mancini to get out of the destroyed SUV. He's sitting firm in the car. He must be waiting for his men to bring him word that I've been killed or captured. "Fuck," I grumble at his refusal to get out of the car. I pull away from the scope and reach for one of the Glocks I have laid out beside my rifle. "South, eighty yards," I instruct Ben.

He lifts his gun and waits. They come at us simultaneously, and both go down simultaneously too. "Three more are right there," Agent says.

Ben and I take them down without them releasing a single round from their weapons, but I know that now we've been exposed. I turn again to peer through my scope. Mancini gets out of the car, giving me the one clear shot I have. I don't have time to set up properly, so I take a deep breath and fire, hoping to hit him. The bullet impacts his leg above the knee, taking him down like a bag of useless shit.

The rest of his men scatter. I quickly fold in my rifle and stand to my feet. "Move," I yell at Ben as I pick up the weapon and start making my way down the hill. "We need to get down to him and finish this now."

"Are you going to kill him?" Ben asks.

"First I want him to see Ethan."

"Let me call in the department," he says as we run down toward the house.

"No. He dies today." Running with a sniper rifle isn't easy, but I need to get to my cabin as fast as I can.

"The others have all scattered," Agent says. "I've killed their cell signals, but it means you're approaching the dead zone. I won't be able to inform you."

I take my earpiece out and shove it into my pocket as we slowly approach the cabin. "Agent's killed the area. We're in a dead zone."

"What?" Ben asks as we approach Mancini, who's now squirming in pain while trying to drag himself toward the SUV for cover.

I take my earpiece out of my pocket and hold it up to Ben. "Dead zone. No service. So, I need you to keep a careful eye out. There are still five more out there who'll likely come for us." With my sniper rifle in my hand I walk over to Mancini and stand over him as he attempts to get away from me. "You look like shit, Tony," I say as I watch his face contort with pain.

"Do you have any idea what I'm going to do to you? I'm going to destroy you, you fucking bitch," he groans through gritted teeth.

I let a laugh escape from me. "I'm so scared," I taunt. I squat down beside him and pat his trembling body down to make sure he doesn't have any weapons. "Would you like to see your son?"

"What have you done to him?" Mancini asks as he gasps through the pain.

I stand and grab Mancini around the collar to drag him inside while Ben stands rigid and watches our surroundings in case the others return. "Fuck you're a heavy piece of shit, aren't you?" I ask as I heave to drag him into my cabin. Although he's like deadweight, I still manage to drag him in through to my room and into the bathroom.

"Tony!" Mancini erupts when he sees his son's lifeless body with a bullet hole between his eyes.

I hear gunfire outside, so I dump Mancini and run outside. I reach Ben who hands me my Glock with his left hand while his right one is up and pointing behind the front SUV. I run ahead, squat beside the tire, and look under the car. I see two sets of feet, so I shoot them both out. The men collapse as they scream in agony. Now I have a clear shot of their heads, and I put a bullet through each of their brains. I see Ben has taken another out, which leaves us with just two more.

I look back to Ben and hold up two fingers before standing and using the SUVs as my shield. Ben ducks down and runs behind the second SUV so we can come around and ambush the two remaining. There are gunshots from over to the right, and I look for Ben to make sure he's safe. With his back to the SUV, he looks over to me and gives me a small nod. More gunshots fly at us, but it gives me the chance to pinpoint where they're coming from. Ducking down, I run around the SUV and disappear into the shrubs, using them for cover while I quickly and quietly make my way over toward the gunmen.

I manage to sneak up behind them and put bullets in the backs of their heads. "Fucking idiots," I say as I walk back to my cabin.

I take my earpiece out, and pop it in my ear. Agent is online by the time I'm walking into my house with Ben by my side. "They're all taken down."

"I know," I reply. "Get Cleaner out here to sort all of this out."

"Do you want me to send Doctor for you?"

"I'm fine." I stop short of my bedroom and look over my shoulder to Ben. I press my earpiece before lowering my chin. "It's best if you stay out here," I say to Ben.

"Let me take him in," Ben says. "Who's this cleaner person?"

"No, I'm ending this now. If I let you take him in, then we're both as good as dead. It ends with me, here."

Ben chews on the inside of his cheek as he contemplates this next move. He takes a step backward and finally nods. "You said something about a cleaner."

"Not a cleaner, *Cleaner*. He's on my payroll, and he cleans up after me when I need him to."

There's a long pause as I wait for Ben to say something to me; instead, he merely runs his hand through his hair. "Both Mancini and Ethan will simply disappear, won't they?"

"Cleaner will see to it that neither are ever found. This house will be flattened with nothing left for anyone to scavenge or find."

Ben looks around and lifts his brows. "Just like that?"

"Just like that," I confirm.

"And you disappear?" He steps closer and reaches out to run is hand down my arm.

My skin pebbles as I suck in a breath and look down at where he's touching me. "I still have something to take care of."

"What?"

I step away from Ben and look over toward the bathroom. "Once Mancini is dead, then there's still one more target on you, and I'm going to have to put them down too."

"When does this stop, Anna?"

I snicker as I look over toward the bathroom again. "Stop?" I shake my head. "This never ends, Ben. This has been my life since I was fifteen."

He steps closer toward me, but I back away from him. I can't let my heart take over, not in this vulnerable moment when I still have work to do. "Anna."

I shrug away from him. "I have to deal with Mancini," I say as I walk away from Ben.

"Anna..."

I head into the bathroom where Mancini is looking pale and haggard. "You look like shit, Tony," I say to him as I lay a swift kick into his leg.

He cries out in pain as he leans his head against the wall. Mancini opens his eyes and looks over my shoulder to glare at Ben. "I should've killed you when I had the chance." I hear Ben's heavy breathing from behind me. "I'm going to tear your entire family apart and send them back to you one piece of flesh at a time."

I smirk as I tap my gun against my thigh. "Dead men can't give orders."

The bullet shoots past me before I have a chance to lift my own gun and put Mancini down. Ben's hard stance and evil glare tells me how much he's hurting. He's staring at Mancini as if he's expecting him to rise from the dead, and he's ready to shoot him again. I place my hand over his and lower the gun. Ben's eyes are wide as he continues to stare at a dead Mancini.

A part of me didn't want blood on Ben's hands, but I'm glad he did it, because he'll be able to put that part of his past behind him.

Ben finally lowers his weapon and steps backward. His hard stance softens as his shoulders sink forward. I step toward him and place my hand over his. I use my body to shield the destruction from Ben and gently guide him into the bedroom. "I've got this," I say. "Go."

I'm surprised to find Ben's lack of emotional reaction. Maybe because he's a cop and he's seen this stuff in the past, but I'm wondering how many dead people he's seen while in Bankstown Creek. This town doesn't have a high crime or gun violence rate—or it didn't until I got here. Perhaps killing Ethan's brother desensitized him. He's clearly grappling with something. I'm curious as to what it is.

Possibly there's more to Ben than meets the eye.

Ben finally relinquishes the weapon to me, sighs once, and heads out to the kitchen. I turn back to the bathroom, and put another bullet into Mancini's chest. When I'm satisfied that they're both dead, I go into my bedroom and pack a bag. I walk out to find Ben standing in the kitchen against the counter. "Are you okay?"

He lifts a bottle of water to his mouth and slowly sips on it. He lowers the bottle and places it on the counter. He finally nods before looking at me. "All these years I thought they died because of a car accident, now I find out they died because I didn't take a bribe." He intakes a breath as his nod changes to a shake. "I'm responsible."

"No, you're not. Mancini is...was," I quickly correct myself. "We've righted a wrong." My phone rings and I touch my earpiece. "Agent."

"Cleaner is en route to the cabin, he'll be there within two hours."

I hang up and look to Ben. "We've got to go. But I need to clear out my weapons room." I search for my keys and hand them to Ben. "Can you bring the car up to the front door?"

He reaches out to take them and skims his fingers across the back of my hand. "Thank you, Anna."

My stomach jumps with excitement as our eyes remain locked on one another. But I need to stay focused because there's still one more assassin I need to take care of. I pull my hand back and walk away from Ben.

For now, I need to concentrate.

CHAPTER THIRTEEN

—•—

"Dad," I say as we drive toward the shooting range.

"Yeah?" Dad places his elbow on the window ledge and keeps an eye on the road.

I play with the ends of my hair as I try to broach the subject without him shutting down. He doesn't like it when I talk about *her*. "Mom left me in the hospital, right?"

Dad straightens and places both hands on the wheel. His fingers tighten until his knuckles are white and he gulps nervously several times. "She did."

"I know you don't like talking about her, but I'm nearly fourteen and I'm really curious about her."

Dad shifts on the bench seat of his truck and he takes a breath. "What do you want to know?" his voice is still strong, but also fragile, like he's really uncomfortable talking to me about it.

"What was she like?"

"She was…" He slowly lifts his shoulders and glances over at me. "She was…" he repeats without adding anything else to it. "She wasn't happy," he finally says.

"Why? Because of me?" I stare down at the floor of the truck, hoping she didn't leave because of me.

"Um." Dad lifts his hand off the wheel to run it through his hair.

"Oh," I whisper. Dad's reaction is all the confirmation I need. "Right."

"Your mother wasn't happy for a long time."

"She's not my mother," I say in a coarse, tight voice. "She's merely a person who carried and gave birth to me."

"She's still your mother, Anna," Dad whispers. There's a moment of tension in the truck while Dad continues toward the range. "I think she struggled with everything in her life."

"Did she come from a traumatic childhood?"

"I don't know," he responds earnestly. "She never talked about herself as a kid or a young woman. She was always so closed off."

"What did you see in her?"

Dad clears his throat. "Wow, I wasn't expecting that from you."

"You've taught me to always be honest. Why would this be any different? But if you don't want to talk about her, we don't have to."

"No, you're asking questions and it's been wrong of me to not answer them in the past." He glances toward me and smiles. "I fell in love with her soft brown eyes and kind smile."

"Did she not love you back?"

"She said she did," he answers sadly.

"Then it was me she didn't want." My palms start sweating, so I rub them over the thighs of my jeans. I turn to look out the window, refusing to let Dad see the tears prickling my eyes. "Did she ever tell you she didn't want me?" my voice cracks, but I do everything I can to hold it together.

"Anna, look at me." Dad leans across to take my hand in his. I pull it away and tuck it under my armpit, not wanting him to touch me. "Anna," he says in a smaller voice. "I wanted you and that should count for something."

A tear rolls down my cheek, and I quickly wipe it away. "She didn't love me, Dad."

"I don't think she ever really loved me either," he admits.

I turn to look at him, and find Dad's eyes are glassy as he holds his own tears in. "I love you," I say.

"That's all that matters, sweetheart."

I choke back the hurt in the base of my throat and link Dad's and my fingers together. "Why did she really leave?"

He pulls into the range and parks the truck, then turns to look at me. "Do you want the honest truth?"

"It's all I ever ask for."

"The truth is, I don't know. She had you and I left to come home and shower and change, and when I returned to the hospital, she was gone. She'd left nothing but a scribbled note written on a scrap of paper. I searched everywhere for her, but I never found her."

"What do you think happened to her?"

Dad slowly lifts his shoulders. He lowers his chin and stares into his lap. "I've spent many a day and night thinking about what could possibly have happened. Truthfully, darling, I have no idea where she is or even if she's alive."

"Dad..."

"I've beat myself up so many times wondering if I could've done something...anything to change her decision to leave." His chest deflates as he sinks further down into the bench seat. "Maybe if I was a better man..."

"No, don't say that. You're a good dad, and I can't imagine you would've been a bad husband." It's clear this has cast a painful cloud over Dad. I look over his shoulder toward the entrance of the shooting range. "Come on, let's go shoot some targets." I force myself to slide out of the car and walk around to Dad's door. I could kick myself for asking about *her*. It's clear Dad is still hurting even after all these years. I open the door and wait for

Dad to grab his gun case and climb out. "Will you teach me to shoot with two hands?"

Dad wipes at his cheeks, then drapes his arm over my shoulders and brings me in for a hug. He kisses the side of my head. "I'm not great at shooting left-handed, but I think Gerald is left-handed, so he'll be able to help you."

"Cool, I'll ask him." The mood between us lightens as we walk into the store part of the shooting range. Gerald is serving a customer and looks up to see who's entered. "Hey, Gerald," I call as I wave at him.

His face lights up when he sees Dad and me. "There are two of my favorite people. Buck, take over," he calls to one of his employees. He walks over to where Dad and I are standing and he looks me up and down. "I swear, kiddo, you get taller every time I see you."

"You have to say that," I say with a cheeky smile.

"Nope, I don't. Anyway, are you both here to use the range?"

"I'm gonna grab myself a coffee," Dad says as he walks over to where the pot's brewing.

"Actually, I have a small favor to ask, Gerald."

"What is it, kiddo?"

"Can you teach me to shoot left-handed please?"

"Sure. We'll start off with a Glock and work our way up. Let me grab my gun." He innocently pats me on the shoulder before walking to his office.

"Is Gerald going to help?" Dad asks as he walks over, sipping his coffee.

"Yeah, he's getting his gun."

"Great." He thrusts the gun case at me. "You know the drill."

"I know." I take the case and head over to the counter. Opening it up, I take both guns out and lay them on the countertop.

"I'm ready when you are, kiddo." Gerald stands beside me and watches. "Safety first."

I pull both Dad's and my gun apart, making sure they're clean and appear to be in good working order. "Dad would kill me if I didn't inspect the gun before I use it."

"Yep, I would," Dad echoes from behind me as he drinks his coffee. He turns to Buck, who's now finished with the customer and he begins talking with him.

"You know, out of all the years I've owned this shooting range, I've never met someone who's so skilled at such a young age. You should consider going into competitions."

"I'm not interested in competitions, Gerald. I do this because I love doing it. And, I'm good at it too." I smirk as I glance sideways at him.

"Yes, you are." I finish with the guns and turn to look at him. "You ready?"

"Sure am."

"Let's go, kiddo."

We head out to the range so he can give me a lesson in shooting with my left hand.

I get out of the shower and start toweling myself dry. I gasp when I see blood between my legs. "Dad!" I yell as I wrap a clean towel around my body and take off out of the bathroom. "Dad!"

"In the kitchen," Dad replies from downstairs. "Is it another spider?" I run down the stairs and stop inside the kitchen, waiting for him to look at me. He turns and steps closer to me. "What is it?" Dad knits his brows together and quickly looks over my body. "Are you hurt?"

"No, nothing like that. Dad, I got my period for the first time and I don't have anything. Can you go to the store and get me pads and tampons."

Dad smiles warmly and draws me in for a hug. "Awww, darling. Hang on a minute." He disappears upstairs to his bedroom where I can hear him stomping with his heavy footsteps. He then walks back down the stairs. "I've been preparing for this day, because obviously I knew it was coming." He hands me a paper bag. "I've got everything I think you'll need. I had to ask Doris down at the store what girls need when it's..." He clears his throat and keeps looking down at the bag. "...that time of the month. And, she showed me what her girls use. I hope this is enough. If not, I can go and buy you something else," he quickly adds.

I open the bag and find an array of tampons and pads, even some Tylenol to help. "Dad," I say as I smile. "You did this?"

"I'm sorry you don't have a mom who can help with this sort of stuff. And, I'm trying not to make it weird or anything, but I really don't know much about this. I'll try better. Just tell me what you need and I'll go right now to get it."

I place the bag on the counter and hug Dad. "Thank you for being you. You're the best dad ever." I step back and take the bag upstairs. Sitting on the edge of my bed I empty the bag and rustle through it. I love Dad so much.

Chapter Fourteen

M y sleep has been shit for a few days now, and last night was no
exception. I turn on the water in the shower in Ben's bathroom,
strip off, and step inside. I close my eyes as I lean my forehead against the
wall, allowing the hot water to pound over my body.

I don't hear Ben. Instead, I sense him. His body presses against mine
while his mouth peppers kisses over my shoulder. Ben stops kissing me
and traces a few old wounds on my back with the tip of his finger. I hate
being reminded of my weaknesses, the times I was wounded because I let
my guard down for a moment.

I turn in Ben's arms to look into his eyes. He lifts his hand to gently touch
my bruised face. "I don't like seeing these marks on you," he says.

"They were necessary so I could get free of Ethan and get the information
I needed."

"You don't have to do this." Ben leans in and kisses my forehead.

I lift my leg to hook around his hip. "It's what I know how to do." I line
his hardening cock up with my pussy and hover over the tip. "And I'm good
at it." He pushes into me, momentarily stopping me from talking.

"You can have a life here, with me," he whispers. "A normal life with me."

"Normal?" I pause and shake my head. "What's even normal?"

"A life with me. You can move in here, be with me. We can do things other normal couples do."

His hips move with mine. Together we're playing a perfect role of happily ever after. "There's nothing normal about me, Ben."

He silences me with his mouth, dragging a long kiss out of me. I shut my eyes to be in the moment, though Ben's words are sending a wave of havoc through my mind. Sunsets, beaches, family and happiness have never been in my vocabulary. They're not my future. Hell, I'll be lucky if I make it to my forties. Ben snakes his hand down between us to bring me to the edge. Ben absorbs my whimpers with his mouth. "We could learn to be normal," he whispers against my lips. "Together." My arms cling around Ben and my body braces as his cock sinks into my desperate pussy. Ben holds me as my pussy pulsates around him. "That's it, squeeze me hard," he groans.

My nails claw at his back while we move together. "More," I moan. "Harder." Ben increases his tempo while his thumb massages my clit. "I'm close."

Ben lowers my leg and pulls out of me. He drops to his knees in the shower, pushes me backward, and feasts on me. His slippery tongue is amazing as his mouth glistens from both the water and my juices. I push my fingers through his hair to keep him in place so he can make me come. "Fuck, you taste like my last meal," he grumbles as he launches forward to keep eating.

I smirk as I concentrate on the magic of his mouth. "There." I force his head to stay where he is. "That's it, right there." Ben is working me with his mouth, while his tongue flicks, licks, and laps at me. "I'm coming," I groan as I grip his hair to keep him from moving. Ben's slurping is pushing me over the edge. My heart rate increases and my body convulses with ecstasy.

My fingers relax as my body calms. Ben stands, tugs onto my right leg and hoists it up over his hip. He rams into me while pinning me against the shower wall. "My turn," he groans. I pull him down and kiss him, tasting a mixture of me and him. "Fuck." His own hips gain speed and within a moment he leans his forehead against mine as he grunts his own release. Our bodies slow as the water keeps pounding at us. Ben's ragged breath eases. He kisses my nose, then releases my leg. "This is what normal people do, Anna."

I was lost in the moment, but he's managed to remind me that I'll never know what normal is. I turn us so he's under the stream of water, giving me the chance to back away. "I lost normal when I was fifteen." I walk out of his shower and grab a towel off the hook.

All this talk of stability is only making me more painfully aware that I'll never have it.

I leave the bathroom and stand in his bedroom, looking at myself in the mirror. I look toward the bathroom, then back at the mirror. "You have a job to do, don't fuck it up," I remind myself.

Once I've killed the other assassin sent for Ben, I have to leave. I can't stay here. Ben is dangerous to me, and I to him. Assassins don't get a chance at happily ever after, not in my world.

"Have you found out who's on their way for Ben?" I ask Agent as I sit on a barstool at the counter while Ben prepares breakfast.

"All I know is what I've given you. They're from Hunter Inc. No one is willing to talk."

"Fuckers," I grumble.

"Cleaner has removed the trash, and he's working on destroying the cabin." Agent chuckles. "He complained."

"About what?"

"The bulletproof glass, the reinforced steel. He said, and bear in mind he said this, not me, 'When is 15 ever going to have a normal house that doesn't take me days to tear apart?' I told him he's more than welcome to speak with you about that issue. He said no fucking way." Agent laughs again.

"What's the ETA on the cabin being destroyed?"

"Cleaner is working on it."

"I don't like ambiguous answers, Agent. I want to know where I stand," I say firmly.

"I'll get an ETA and let you know. I'm also chasing any lead I can get to find who the assassin is, and their weakness. Doctor is in Bankstown Creek too, in case he's needed for anything." Good, I usually try to keep him as close to me as possible, because I never know when I'll need him. Although, the number Ethan did on me will heal on its own, over time.

I disconnect the call and take my earpiece out. I toss it on the counter beside my phone. "Everything okay?" Ben asks as he continues with breakfast.

"What are you making?" I actively avoid his question.

"I'm making us pancakes with real maple syrup. Coffee should be ready soon." He flips a pancake, then turns back to me. "Everything okay?" he repeats.

"I guess you need to know what's happening." I chew on my lower lip and take a breath. "Agent can't find who's coming for you."

"Tell me about these people you have working for you."

"What do you want to know?"

"Who's Agent? Cleaner? Who are they?"

"I have a team of people on my payroll. They work only for me, and they do whatever it is I ask of them, no questions asked."

"How do you know they can be loyal?"

"Because they've seen me work, and they don't want me as an enemy. They know the consequences if they betray me."

"Which is?"

"I'll kill them, and everyone in their family."

Ben's brows rise as he looks down at the counter. The coffee machine clicks off, and silently, he turns and pours us coffees. He brings mine over and places it on the counter. "Do you kill just anyone?"

"As in do I have *standards*?"

"Exactly. Or do you kill anyone you're hired to kill?" He sips on his coffee as he watches me.

"I have standards, Ben. I don't kill kids, and I won't just walk up to someone and shoot them. I'm not a psychopath."

Ben's lips tug at the side. "Okay, so you're not a psychopath." He chuckles and shakes his head. "I feel like there's so much I need to know about you."

"You know my biggest secret. I have nothing else to hide."

Ben sets his mug on the counter and returns his attention to the pancakes. He slides some off the griddle and hands me a plate with four pancakes. "There's more." He quickly grabs flatware and slides them across the counter to me. "Your father is Harry Brookes, and all I know is he was murdered in a house fire."

"Our home was built right here." I cut into the stack of fluffy pancakes. "Right here." I look around his kitchen.

"A few of the older cops told me that when they found out where I lived. How is it for you being back here?"

"At first it was surreal, but this house is nothing like mine." I'm growing more uncomfortable talking about Dad and our home. It's not a memory I want to relive.

Ben senses my difficulty in talking about Dad and thankfully changes the course of our conversation. "How many people do you have working for you?"

"Less than a handful. They all have certain jobs they're good at, and I pay them well to look after me when I need them to."

"How much did Mancini pay you to kill me?"

My hand stills because I knew this question was coming. I look up at him and swallow what's in my mouth. "Two million down and one million more when the job was complete."

Ben's fingers tighten around his mug before turning away. "Three million?"

"Everyone has a price, Ben."

"What would your price be?"

"There's a bounty on my head," I say matter-of-factly.

Ben pivots and does a double take. "There's a bounty out for you?" I nod. "Who? Why?"

"Ronan Murphy put a price on my head back when his henchmen originally tried to take me. But I killed them both before they got too far."

"Do you know what the bounty is?"

"Why? Are you going to kill me and claim it?"

A closed-lip smile tugs at his mouth. "Maybe. What's it worth?"

I sit back on the stool and cross my arms in front of my chest. Cocking an eyebrow, I silently warn him. "No idea."

He holds his hands up in playful surrender. "Don't worry, I'm not going to kill you."

A massive laugh escapes from me. "It's cute you even think you could."

His pancakes are now on his plate. He turns to face me and starts cutting into them. "You're like a female James Bond. Or maybe one of Charlie's Angels."

"Except I kill people for money," I point out the obvious difference between me and all those characters who are fundamentally good people. "There's nothing wholesome about me."

"I wouldn't say that. You could've killed me, but you didn't."

"That's because I didn't get that feeling I get."

"What feeling?" Ben asks as he continues to eat his pancakes.

I push my plate away, done with breakfast. "The best way I can describe it is that it's like a sixth sense. I get this feeling about someone when I touch them. I know instantly if someone is who I've been told they are."

His brows scrunch together. "That's not exactly very scientific."

"I never said it was, but it's also never failed me. I heavily rely on my senses, and if it feels like something isn't right, then I *know* something isn't right."

"Did you get that feeling when you first met me?"

"Nope."

"Good to know."

"Are you hiding something I should know about?"

"I have a safe room in my basement."

"Why do you have a safe room?" This piques my interest.

"Because I'm the police chief, and one day I'm hoping to have a family. I built a safe room to protect them in case anything ever happened. I'm safeguarding my future." I purse my lips together as I stare at Ben. The reply is feasible, but suspicious too. "How many people have you killed?"

I'm still questioning why he has a safe room in his house. I worry my lower lip between my teeth as I carefully watch him. "A lot," I reply coldly. "Where's your safe room?"

"In the basement," he says. "Want me to show you?"

"What's the code?"

"Seven-seven-three-four-nine."

"You gave that to me easily."

"I have nothing to hide. I'll take you down there right now and show you." He walks over toward a door that leads down to the basement. "I have enough supplies to last nearly a week down there."

"You don't have to show me, I believe you."

Ben returns to the kitchen and lifts his mug. "Will you tell me now how many people you've killed?"

"No."

"Why?"

"Because the number differs."

"How so?"

"There are paid kills and there are the others who've gotten in my way so I had to take care of them."

"Like Mancini's men?"

"And Mancini, and Ethan. But yes, like them."

"Have you killed over a hundred people?" My brows rise as I struggle to hold in the chuckle. "A hundred and fifty?"

I shake my head as I move to lean my elbows on the counter. "Honestly, you don't want to know, Ben. Besides, I don't keep track of the number."

Ben blinks rapidly and rubs at the tension across his forehead. "More than a hundred and fifty?"

"You don't get to be at my level with only a few kills."

Suddenly, the family room window explodes and I see Ben fly backward to hit the floor with a massive thud. I fly out of my chair and over the counter to see Ben lying on the floor with blood oozing out of his chest, creating a widening pool around his body.

It takes me no longer than a few seconds to lift my head and grab my phone and earpiece. I call Agent. "Get Doctor here now!" With my bare hands, I tear at his t-shirt to see where the wound is.

"Fuck," Ben groans with pain.

"Shut up and stay still." I roll him over and see that the bullet hasn't come out through his back. "Fuck!" Ben's eyes flutter open and close. "Stay with me." I smack his face, trying to get him to stay awake. His eyes finally close as he takes a final breath. "Ben."

"Doctor is en route now."

"Get him here!" I shout at Agent. "I don't care what you have to do."

I apply pressure to stop the bleeding. It feels like hours have passed. "Doctor is in the driveway."

I take my earpiece out and run toward the front door. With blood covering my hands, I open the door to Doctor, who's hauling a rolling suitcase behind him and carrying a black doctor's bag. "Situation?"

I lead him into the kitchen where Ben is on the floor. "Bullet to the chest, no exit wound. I've been trying to stop the bleeding."

"I'll resuscitate while you apply pressure. Do you have somewhere I can operate on him?"

"I do."

"Where is it?" He scoops Ben up as I run ahead toward his safe room. I find it in the basement and with the code he told me earlier, I open the door, then Doctor forges ahead. There's a table and Doctor places Ben on it. "I need my bags." I run upstairs to grab his suitcase and doctor's bag, and in the meantime, Doctor has removed his hat and his coat and has his sleeves rolled up. "Put pressure on the wound. We need to stop the bleeding." Doctor opens his bag and pulls out an extendable IV stand and a bag of fluids. He finds a vein in Ben's arm and inserts a needle into it. I'm still holding my bloody hands over a blood-soaked towel on Ben's chest. Once the IV is set up, Doctor flicks a look up to me. "Go, I've got this."

"Don't let him die," I warn.

Doctor lifts his gaze and arches a brow. "I've got this," he repeats.

I take a step back and watch as he works on Ben. I find myself fighting murderous thoughts. My pulse is thumping as adrenaline rushes through my body. I'm going to find the person who did this to Ben and I'm going to tear them apart, limb from fucking limb. My hands tremble and my jaw tightens as I grind my teeth together.

"If you need anything, call Agent," I say to Doctor, who's got surgical tweezers in Ben's chest. "I'm locking you in for your own protection. Keep him alive and you'll be substantially rewarded." He doesn't even acknowledge my statement. He just keeps working on Ben. I close and lock the door before I run upstairs and wash the blood off of my hands. I need a moment to clear my anger and think logically, not emotionally.

I head into the kitchen. There's blood everywhere, instantly reminding me of how I failed to keep Ben safe. I can't help but ball my hands into fists as rage fills every fiber of my being. I close my eyes and breathe deeply. Calming my rage is paramount, or I'll end up getting myself killed by making a move before I've seen the whole picture.

I snap my eyes open, feeling calmer and more focused. I need to find whoever did this, and kill them. Turning my back on the destruction, I go to the bedroom, to my bag, and take my laptop out. I tap my earpiece for Agent. "Is he okay?" Agent asks.

"Doctor's working on him."

"What do you need?"

"I noticed Ben has security cameras around the outside of his house. I need you to patch me into the feed." I cross my legs on the bed and watch as Agent accesses my laptop and brings the camera views up. "How far back does this go?"

"It's constantly recording, you'll be able to go back as far as...hang on, let me check." There's a few keystrokes on his end before he says, "Looks like it's set to record over at the end of every week."

"Good." I hang up and navigate the feed. My goal is to see who fired that shot, find them, and take them out. I lean closer to the screen as I near the time of the shooting. A hooded figure appears just out of range of focus. I dial Agent again. "Can you clear the image up on the screen?"

I take the laptop off my lap and place it on the bed and quickly retie my hair into a ponytail. Agent is nothing short of the best technician when it comes to anything to do with technology. He can hack, create, build or even destroy just about anything electronic.

"Camera quality isn't the best. Give me a second, let me see who else has cameras set up on their premises." The screen in front of me pauses but I can hear him doing whatever he does. "One of the neighbors down the road is super weird." Agent snorts a chuckle. "Tell me you're paranoid without telling me you're paranoid."

"Hurry up," I snap at him.

A heavy quiet settles over us as I wait for him to do his thing. "This is the clearest I can get the image. It's still grainy, but maybe you can figure out who this is."

The picture flicks up on my laptop. I lean forward and focus in on the image on the screen. All the air leaves my lungs as I slump and continue to stare at the person on the screen. "What the fuck..."

Chapter Fifteen

—◆—

Past

My hit has yet to come into view through the scope. I lay on my stomach, patiently waiting for the target. "Yeah," I say as I touch my earpiece.

"I've found something."

I keep watching through the scope, waiting for the woman to emerge. "And you're calling me now to tell me this?" I say dismissively. How important could whatever he found actually be?

"I know you're on a hit, but, you told me you wanted to know the moment I had news," Agent says.

I blink a moment and move my head back. "Did you find her?" Agent knows never to distract me with anything frivolous, so I know this means he's finally been able to track her down.

"I did."

My teeth sink into my bottom lip as I think for a moment. Physically finding my mother wasn't something I thought could ever happen because a big part of me was hoping she was dead. "Where is she?" I ask in a small, cracking voice.

"She's in a rehab facility."

She's a junkie? I'm not even surprised. I purse my lips together and look through the scope again. I touch my earpiece, disconnecting the call from Agent. I have to think about this, and what I want to do about it.

It was a few years back when I decided I needed to know where she is. I had Agent search for her through public records, and we found her name but never managed to actually find her. *Until now.*

Fuck. My mind isn't focused, and I can't miss this hit. I don't get paid the big bucks to fail. I push all thoughts of my mother out of my mind and pay attention on the target.

The sun reflecting down makes the top of the asphalt-roofed building hotter than what the day actually is. The air ripples heat waves as I continue to look through the scope, waiting for the target to emerge from her building.

I can't afford to be rattled by the news.

No, I need to have laser focus.

I pull my attention away from the scope again and look down at the mat I've laid on the hot rooftop. I'll have to deal with my mother once this hit has been completed. *Get yourself together, 15.* I close my eyes for a few seconds and take several deep breaths to calm myself. Once I'm in control of myself, I snap my eyes open and look into the scope again. I touch my earpiece. "What's the ETA on the target?"

"She's walking through the lobby now."

My finger rests over the trigger as I keep a steady eye on the front door. A black car rolls to a stop at the front of the building, and the driver stays firmly in the car. A man dressed in a black suit exits the building and holds his hand up to whoever is following him. He takes a moment to glance around before proceeding to the car and opening the back door. He gestures toward someone from the building to head out.

Another man in a black suit follows. He, too, carefully checks his surroundings.

A young woman and her daughter are walking along the sidewalk and happily cross where the two men are. The second man holds his hand up to stop the next procession of security walking out until the woman and her daughter have passed.

Good. I don't want the kid to see what a head splattered clear off the shoulders of a person looks like. The mother and the kid slow their walk and hover outside a store front.

"Move," I say to myself. I know the target is about to emerge, but I can't do it if there's a kid standing near her. "Come on." My forearms strain as sweat beads across my hairline. "Leave." My mouth dries and my pulse quickens.

The target strolls out of the building. Her oversized sunglasses do nothing to conceal her notorious hard stare. She's a human trafficker who's created a stir by not staying in her lane. She's also attempting a hostile takeover of the *dis*honorable Antonio DeLuca. Her foray into crossing a mob boss is what is leading, ultimately, to her own demise. Antonio DeLuca is a hard fucker, completely unrelenting. Smiley came straight out of the gate thinking she can overtake a business that's been in operation for generations.

Stupid fucking name she's given herself, and completely ironic too. I'm not even sure she knows how to smile.

I'm going to have to find another way to take her down, because I refuse to cause that kind of trauma to the kid. I glance at the mom and see she takes her kid by the hand and ducks inside the store.

I look at the target and smirk. I still have time to do this.

I follow her path from the building to the car, and with less than a few yards before she enters the car, I adjust the iron sight by six clicks, then squeeze the trigger. Within seconds, Smiley is no longer alive. Her security detail ducks for cover while they frantically yell and scream. One of her men is covered in Smiley's brain matter.

I keep a watch as the security guards finally stand and look around them. I can't help but chuckle at their disbelief. "Seriously, boys?" I say as I shake my head and finally start breaking down my sniper rifle. My earpiece buzzes once and I touch it before I continue taking my rifle apart. "Yeah."

"Nice shot. When I saw the kid I thought you were going to call it off," Agent says.

"Yeah, I was going to, but the mom took the kid into the store and it gave me the opportunity I needed."

"I've already let the employer know the hit's been completed. He's initiated the transfer."

"Good." I open the duffel bag and shove the body of the rifle into it. "Where's the facility?" I ask as I pause packing the rifle away.

"Arizona."

"Arizona?" I grumble. "Get me on a flight there and find out what her drug of choice is."

"You're going to meet her?" Agent is just as surprised as I am by my request.

I swallow the tightness in my throat and continue packing the rifle. "I don't know. Just, get me on a flight." I hang up, stand, and take the duffel with me as I make my way down the building and to my car.

I open the trunk of the car and place the duffel inside it before closing the lid. Once inside the car, I sit behind the wheel and stare ahead of me. There are sirens rushing past the parking garage as they make their way toward the hotel where Smiley's body is lying on the sidewalk.

A part of me wants to confront my mother, but another part wants her to die for abandoning my father and me. I'll deal with that internal conflict when I get to Arizona.

I never in a million years thought I'd be standing outside a rehab center, nervous about confronting my mother. She abandoned us, and now she's paid the price for that sin by becoming a dirty fucking junkie. She brought this on herself; she's reaping what she sowed.

It takes me what feels like forever to finally gain the courage to walk into the building. Visiting hours are over soon, but I have to meet her and tell her what a fucked-up thing she did to Dad and me.

"Hi," a young nurse greets with a smile and a pleasant tone. I look around and don't reply to her. "Can I help you?"

"You have a patient I'd like to see."

"Who's the patient?" She looks toward the computer and waits for me to give her Natalia's name. She types it into the system, and I watch as she reads the notes attached to the file. "Natalia was only just admitted this week for rehabilitation."

"I'd like to see her."

"I need to speak with one of her doctors first."

"You do that. I'll wait."

"Are you a relative of the patient?"

Yeah, the gutless fucker abandoned me and my father only hours after I was born. "No, I'm not."

"I'm sorry, but in the first two weeks of treatment we only allow relatives and next of kin to visit with the patients."

That rule has just saved Natalia's life. I truly believe I would've killed her if I had the opportunity. It's the reason I'm here. I have a fatal dose of heroin ready to inject stashed in my pocket.

Natalia lives to see another day.

For now.

CHAPTER SIXTEEN

After a few hours of shut-eye, my mind is clear and sharp. I know what I have to do, and this ends today. I walk down to where Doctor and Ben are and open the door. "How's he doing?" I ask Doctor as I flick my gaze to Ben.

"He'll live," Doctor replies flatly. "I'll stay with him until he wakes, which will likely be over the next day or so. I've called Agent and given him a list of supplies I need. They'll be delivered sometime today."

I fold my arms in front of my chest while I nod my understanding. "How bad was it?"

"Half an inch to the left and we'd be having a different conversation."

"When he's awake, help him up the stairs and then you can leave." Doctor arches a brow but finally nods once. "I have work to do." I take off up the basement stairs. First thing I have to do is call Agent. "Find out who's running Hunter Inc. now."

"Doctor said Ben will be okay," Agent says.

"Have you got that name for me yet?" I don't want to talk about Ben or what Doctor has said to Agent.

"Accessing that information now. Current owner of Hunter Inc. is Lincoln Murphy." *Fuck.* He's unpredictable and more ruthless than his father.

He's bloodthirsty and will absolutely run Hunter Inc. into the ground. "Sending his number through to your phone now."

I hang up from Agent once I have the information I need and look down at the number on my screen. Fucking Lincoln Murphy is more dangerous than Ronan ever was. He loves violence. I dial the number and wait for him to answer. "What?" he snaps irritated.

"Do you know who this is?" A cold chill of vengeance washes over me.

He chuckles cynically into the phone. "I've been waiting for you to call, 15."

"We need a meeting."

He clicks his tongue several times, drawing this call out. "I'll give you a meeting, only because you did me the favor of getting rid of my father." I'm not even surprised by his cold admission. He was probably trying to work out how he could do it without it looking like he actually did it. "You're currently in Bankstown Creek, I believe." Asshole knows exactly where I am. "It just so happens that I'm nearby. Dinner at six. Bella Luna."

"Six is fine," I reply coldly. My teeth grind together, causing a shooting pain in my jaw. I'm going to make him hurt.

"And don't think I can't have you killed," he warns. "Sorry about that friend of yours, he had such a promising life ahead of him."

"What do I care? He was collateral damage."

Lincoln laughs sarcastically. "I'm sure you have some questions about your mother. She has quite an aim, doesn't she, 15?" he brags patronizingly. I simply disconnect the call. I have a time and a place, and that's all I need for now.

I already hate him with every fiber of my being. He's confirmed to me what I thought, which is that Natalia was the assassin who pulled the trigger on Ben. But now, I have a ton of questions as to how she ended up working at Hunter Inc., and why I didn't know.

All these questions will be answered in good time.

I dial Agent. "I need you to see if Lincoln keeps a digital calendar on where he's going to be."

"I'll hack into his phone." He types on the keyboard. "He has a dinner reservation at some place called Bella Luna from five tonight, then he's at the ballet from eight."

"Ballet?"

"Yeah. Also, he has a meeting scheduled tomorrow morning in Minneapolis but the only information it says is the initial *Y*. There are a few other meetings, but nothing is as cryptic as the *Y*. I'll keep searching and let you know what I find."

"I need the floorplans for Bella Luna."

"I'll send them through in a few moments."

"I also need you to keep an eye on his calendar and let me know if anything changes." I hang up and head back downstairs for a moment before I get the plans for Bella Luna. Doctor is checking Ben's vitals. "Everything okay?"

"Like I said earlier, he's lucky it missed his heart."

I stand beside Ben and run my fingers over his hair as I watch him being cared for by the best surgeon I've ever met. "Luck has nothing to do with it," I say to Doctor.

A well-trained assassin wouldn't have missed that shot. Ben was standing in the same position long enough for the assassin to acquire true aim.

My earpiece pings and I step away from Ben. "What?"

"The floorplans of the restaurant have been sent to your laptop."

I take one final look at Ben and make my way upstairs to my computer. I have a lot of questions about Natalia, but I know they're going to be answered tonight.

One way, or another.

I scope the restaurant for this evening, making a mental note of everything I need to pay attention to in order to ensure my plan is executed successfully. I sit outside the restaurant in my car and open the laptop to pull up the blueprints of the place.

I flick a look at the time in the corner of my laptop's screen, and I know I'll be tight on time, but I have to get this done. I tap my earpiece and wait the two rings for Agent to pick up. "I'm sending you a list of three specific things I need to be sent to the motel where I'm staying."

"The delivery should arrive within the hour."

I hang up and close the laptop. I pull into the street and drive to the closest hardware store to purchase the remainder of the items I need. *All in cash, of course.*

The motel I'm staying in is clean, but also in a part of town that law enforcement doesn't patrol often, so I know I'll be able to work in peace and quiet.

I set everything up and start on what I can get done until Courier arrives with what I need. There's a knock on the door, and I grab my Glock and walk over toward it, making sure I stand off-center just in case Murphy has found out where I am and has sent his goons for me. There's another single knock on the door. "Turn down service," the familiar male voice calls.

I unlock the door, open it, and stand to the side. Courier walks in holding his helmet and hands me a small package wrapped in brown paper. His motorcycle is three bays down and opposite my room. My suspicious mind forces me to scan the parking area and beyond, in case I've been made. "Be careful," I say as I place the package on the table.

Courier gives me a curt nod before leaving.

I have only a few hours to finish this before I have to return to the restaurant for my meeting with Lincoln Murphy.

I close my eyes and take several deep breaths. My skin pebbles with the fear that this may not work. Snapping my eyes open, I hold my head up and leave the motel, ready for this meeting.

Fifteen minutes later, I find a parking space right out in front of the restaurant. Convenient, and I'm sure was planned by him. I chuckle to myself at his predictability. I get out of my car and walk in to the restaurant.

I'm stopped at the door by one of his many goons. "Fuck," I grumble when I look up at him. This guy is stereotypically massive, with no neck and a nasty scowl stuck on his face.

"Boss," he says with a deep gravelly tone.

"You should lay off the cigarettes," I say.

He looks at me and arches a brow as if he's offended by the fact I'm speaking to him. "Pat her down," Lincoln says, clearly doubting that I'm unarmed.

I lift my arms out and the smirking security guy pats me down. He takes his time when he presses his massive hands over my breasts, then my ass and crotch. "If you don't remove your hands from me, I'll be sure to make you scream."

He laughs dismissively as if my threat is empty.

"Please." Lincoln lifts his hand and gestures for me to join him. On a side table, a buffet is laid out. He hands me a plate, then takes one himself and makes his way from dish to dish. "Come, eat." He signals again.

I take my plate and cast an eye over all the food. "For a small man, you certainly eat a lot," I insult not only his stature but also his presence. He stills his fork and looks up to me. "You look so much like Ronan," I patronize him further.

"I'm nothing like that cunt," he spits. I love knowing I've already gotten under his skin. I feed off his contempt for his father. Lincoln lowers his chin for a moment and regroups before lifting his eyes to look at me. He places his fork down and folds his arms in front of his chest. "I'm so rude, I shouldn't use such vulgar language in front of a woman."

A couple of his men snicker. I smile as I mimic his posture. "How's my mother?"

"Wow, so you're eager to get right to it, are you? I thought perhaps we could talk about you for a while."

I roll my eyes and let out a long sigh. "No need." I flick a look to the two men standing behind him and wink at one of them. "Tell me about Natalia."

He laughs with gusto and shakes his head. "You think you can waltz in here and control this meeting?"

"Okay. What do you want?" I ask, cutting to the crux of this meeting.

"I want you."

"Sorry, I'm unavailable."

"It's not a request," he counters with a warning.

I relax back into the chair and cross my legs as I click my tongue to the roof of my mouth. "Well, this isn't going to plan, is it?" I run my tongue along my teeth and smile. "Tell me about Natalia."

He links his fingers together and steeples his pointer fingers, bringing them to his mouth. He taps them on his lips several times, then lowers his hands. "Your mother's talent is out of this world." I feel like choking on my own vomit. She's subpar, at best. "Unfortunately, she's on assignment at the moment and you won't be able to meet her."

Assignment my ass. She's close by. "How did she become involved in this lifestyle, Lincoln?"

He glances at one of his men and shakes his head. These long pauses are killing my head from boredom. I could have killed him ten times over already. "She came at me one night, and tried to kill me."

"Why would she do that?" *Other than the fact you're a fucking idiot.*

"She was strung out, high on drugs, and she came at me with a spoon. Some man approached her when she was shooting up, gave her a couple of hundred dollars, and told her to kill me and he'd give her more money."

"A spoon?" I mean, it can be done, but considering she was a junkie, there's no way she could've thought she'd be successful. "Who wanted you dead?"

"It doesn't matter." Lincoln downturns his lips and half shrugs. "He's gone." He flicks his hand. "But your mother." He smiles warmly as he recalls. "I saw something in her. It's not often anyone can catch me off guard, and I appreciated that in her. So, I took her off the streets, cleaned her up and trained her to be the best assassin in the world." He pulls his shoulders back with pride and admiration. Something tells me she's more to him than just an employee.

"Are you with her?" Now, I'm really going to vomit.

"She's a spectacular woman." Sounds like confirmation to me.

I reach for my phone and his men instantly react to my move. "It's just my phone," I say as I slowly take it out and place it, face up, on the table. Lincoln holds his hand up to his men. "If I took you up on your offer, what would my position be with Hunter Inc.?"

"You'd start at the bottom, of course."

"Of course," I say sarcastically, matching his condescending smugness.

"You'd be at my disposal."

I'm doing everything I can not to laugh in his face. "Uh-huh." I uncross my legs and sit closer to the table. "And, what exactly would you have me doing?"

"You'd have assignments. Though, you'd be answering to Natalia. You don't have a problem with that, do you?"

I could easily put a bullet in all their heads right now, but I'm unarmed. "I do have a problem, Lincoln. Because I'm positive the bounty on my head will never be lifted, which means you'll hold that over me until the day I die."

"If you come to work for me, you'll go through a probationary period, and if you follow all the rules and perform well, I'll lift the bounty then."

How is this guy the head of Hunter Inc.? He has one brain cell and it's bouncing around in that big head of his all by itself. "I see," I *tsk* and look over at the door. "How about this—" I start my offer.

"This isn't a negotiation."

"You and I both know, that's exactly what this is." I purse my lips together as I smile. "Lift the bounty right now, and I'll come work for you."

"The bounty is my insurance against you."

"The bounty is my reason to kill you."

Lincoln's arrogant laugh grates on my nerves, but I have to hold it together long enough to get the job done. "And what makes me believe that once I lift the bounty that you won't get up and leave?"

"Natalia," I say. The sneer quickly disappears. "Her instructions are that unless I agree to your offer that she's to put a bullet in my brain the moment I'm outside. That's why there was a parking spot in front of the restaurant, so you can watch my head being blown off in case I decline your offer. She's across the street. Last window on the left, with the barrel of her gun peeking out from the window. She believes that's the prime sniper position." I lean forward and whisper, "It's not, but we wouldn't want to hurt your or her fragile ego by proving that." I sit back again. "So, humor me. Take the bounty off, and I'll come work for you."

Lincoln sits straighter in his seat, knowing full well that I'm right. She's exactly where I said she is. "I want to pass on my condolences to you for your friend. I do believe you had a special relationship with him," he taunts, attempting to make me lose my cool.

He has no idea how skilled I am.

"He was a stepping stone for me." I shrug as if I'm disinterested. However, I'm thankful Murphy believes Ben is dead.

He leans back into his chair and brings his arms up to rest at the back of his head. "My apologies for insulting your work. You're not as good as your mother, but you're quite adequate at what you do. Nowhere near as refined as Natalia though," he manages to get that little dig in.

"If I'm not talented, then why do you want me so badly?"

"Because I think you have potential. I also think that under the guidance of your mother, you could be quite useful to me."

"Well, I see this only working one way. Lift the bounty, and I'll work for you. Don't, and you'll kill me the moment I'm near my car. If you don't lift the bounty, then I'm dead."

"And you're prepared for that?"

I snicker as I stare at him, then slowly look over my shoulder to where I can see the open window and the gun barrel peeking out. I give Natalia a small wave. "I've been prepared for my death since the day I killed the two goons your father sent after me." I click my tongue and stare at Murphy. "The choice is yours. You remove the bounty and I work for you, or you take me out right now." I bring my hands up and ring them together as I flick my gaze to the two guys in the back, then discreetly down to my phone, then back out to Natalia before returning my attention to Murphy.

He slowly reaches into his pocket and removes his phone. He dials a number and brings the phone to his ear. "The bounty has been cancelled for good."

I repeat the process of looking around the room. Checking my phone to see a text has come through. Agent's been monitoring not only what's happening in the restaurant but also Murphy's phone. This is where the fun is about to start. "It's over?" I ask, feigning my servitude to him.

"It is."

"Good." I stand, sweep my phone off the table, and shove it into my pocket. His two guards rush forward with drawn guns. "Wow, everyone is on edge. Considering I'm an inadequate assassin, that was an over-the-top reaction from your goons, don't you think?" I taunt.

"You have to understand, 15, I need to make an example out of you."

"Do you?" I ask with zero emotion.

"As much as I could use your talents, I need to send a message to anyone who wants to fuck with me that they're disposable. Just like you. Sorry," he responds with equal emotion. "It's just business."

"Yes, it is. Before you kill me, you need to know something."

"What's that?"

"Natalia is nothing in comparison to me. She's so insignificant that I had no idea she was even trying to be an assassin."

Murphy laughs heartily as he shakes his head. "It's such a shame I have to kill you."

I lift my shirt showing him a strip on my ribs that looks like an oversized band-aid. "If you kill me, you'll die too."

Murphy's smile quickly disappears as the color drains from his face. "What's that?"

"This?" I point to the bandage. "A little something I prepared earlier, just for you," I cockily reply. "I thought I'd arrive before you and set a slew of them up all around the restaurant. Want to know what they do?"

Murphy gulps as his eyes dart around the restaurant. His men cock the safeties back on their guns. "What are they?" he asks with a quiver to his voice.

"Bombs." I smile. "This one though, it's my favorite. If Natalia takes the shot and I fall to the ground, this entire restaurant will be annihilated." Murphy bites on his lower lip stopping himself from snarling. "By the way, once I leave, I'd strongly suggest no one use their cell phone. My colleague activated the bombs once you hung up from revoking the bounty. So if you use your cell, then..." I smack my hands together and slowly extend them out, wiggling my fingers. "Boom." I smile. "I have to go now, but thank you for removing the bounty. Oh, and by the way, if, by some miracle, you manage to get out of here alive, I suggest you don't try to reinstitute the bounty. I can get to you, Lincoln, just like I got to your father."

The color has completely drained from his face, leaving him looking like he's about to pass out. "I'm going to fucking kill you," he spits as I walk toward the front door.

"I'd suggest you don't try to leave by the back door."

"Don't touch your fucking phones!" he screams at his team as I leave.

I walk out of the restaurant and look up at the window where Natalia is. I smile and point up at her. When I'm in the car, I look over at Murphy, then back to Natalia. The window where she was has now closed, and I daresay she's hightailing it to get to Murphy.

I merge onto the road and head straight for the motel.

My heart is thumping so hard, because I honestly had no idea if that was going to work or not. What I do know is the bounty is off my head, and now I need to finally end this.

I adjust the scope while making sure my target doesn't move. I touch my earpiece and take a breath. "Has anything changed?"

"I've infiltrated every possible corner of the dark web, and nothing has changed."

That's all I need to know. I hang up and look through the scope. I close my eyes for a moment to calm my mind and heart rate.

Opening my eyes, a sense of relief embraces me. I dial the number and wait for him to answer. He looks at the phone screen and scrunches his brows together. He looks around before answering. "Whoever the fuck this is, you better have a fucking good explanation."

Beside him, Natalia sits straighter and carefully looks around. Pure rage courses through my veins as I stare at the beautiful woman. Her long hair cascades down over her right shoulder in a low side ponytail. Her skin has a perfect glow, like being touched by the sun. Her makeup is flawless, impeccable.

"Say goodbye to your precious Natalia." I release the first bullet for its target. Her entire body jerks backward when the bullet makes contact with her head.

"What the fuck!" Murphy yells.

The commotion in the private circle at the ballet doesn't stop me. "I'm still at the top of this business." One of his men tries to yank him out of the open, but my bullet reaches him before he has a chance to hide.

His men scramble and yell, causing the rest of the ballet audience to search for the source of all the noise. "Ahh!" someone screams. I quickly and quietly break down my rifle and pack it away to make a hasty exit, covered by the frantic stampede of people trying to leave the theater.

See you later, motherfucker.

CHAPTER SEVENTEEN

BEN

"What the fuck," I grumble and try to sit up.

"Don't move," says a man from somewhere in the room.

"Who are you?" I look around to see where I am and easily recognize my safe room. Despite the agony radiating through my body, I manage to turn my head and see a man sitting on a makeshift seat with his feet elevated while he's scrolling through a tablet. With every breath, pain shoots deep into my gut, causing me to moan. "What happened?"

"You were shot," he replies with a shrug and zero fucks given.

"Who are you?"

"I'm Doctor." He doesn't even lift his eyes to look at me.

"Why are you here?"

"You were shot," he replies with a short, curt tone. I try to push up off the bed, but the pain ripping through me is so severe, I barely have enough strength to breath. "Don't try to get up." He finally places the tablet down and flicks a bored look toward me. He stands and walks over to begin checking my vitals.

"How long have I been out?"

"This is day three. You were shot in the chest, and if 15 hadn't called when she did, you'd be dead."

15? It occurs to me that the doctor most likely doesn't know Anna's name and he only knows her as her code name, 15. "Where is she?" My throat is dry and scratchy. "I need some water."

"I'll get you some." He opens one of the bottles of water I have stocked in here and pours it into a paper cup. He brings it over and helps me maneuver upright so I can take a sip.

"Thank you," I whisper as I lay back down. "Where's 15?"

He completely disregards my question and walks over to retake his seat. He takes the tablet and begins scrolling again. "When you're able, I'll help you up the stairs. A nurse has been organized to come assist you until you can move around on your own."

"I don't need a nurse. I need to know where 15 is." My body burns from the pain coursing through it, but I push and push until I finally sit up. My chest is bandaged and I have a drip in my arm. "Who shot me?"

Doctor lifts his eyes and sighs. "I told you not to move."

"Where's my phone? I need to call 15." I'm careful not to say her name.

Doctor heavily sighs and rolls his eyes. "Here." He shoves the phone toward me and returns to his seat and tablet.

I dial Anna's number and find it's been disconnected. I try it again in case I dialed an incorrect number. Again, I'm told the number has been disconnected. "Do you know how to get in contact with her?" Doctor's brows rise, but he otherwise ignores my question.

"Seeing as you're sitting up, I'll assist you upstairs. The nurse is already on the way." He stands and walks over to me, slides his arms under mine, and helps me stand. For an old man, he's certainly strong. It feels like it takes me hours to get up the stairs, and when I do, he helps me over to the sofa. I look around the room and find everything is in place. "15 had the window replaced, and everything's been cleaned."

"Like it never happened," I say. "Do you have a name?"

"Doctor," he replies in a deadpan voice.

"Do you have any other name you go by?"

"Doctor," he repeats in the same toneless voice. As I lay on the sofa, he disappears down into the safe room before returning with a bag in each hand. "Do what the nurse tells you to do, and you'll be fine." He looks out the window, then back to me. "Nurse will be here soon." He stares at me for a moment, then walks out the front door.

I try dialing Anna once more before letting my phone fall by my leg. "Fuck," I grumble. My phone rings, and although the pain is intense, I reach for it in hopes Anna is calling. "Hey," I say without checking the number.

"Where have you been?" Emily, my sister, asks.

"I got shot."

"What? Where are you? I'm coming to you."

"No, don't. I'll be fine."

"What happened? Thomas, put on the TV and check the news, Ben was shot," she shouts to her husband.

"It didn't make the news, Emily. And, no, don't come to me. I'm fine."

"What happened?"

Shit, my mind isn't clear enough to make up an excuse yet. "Look, I'm really tired, can we talk about my injury later?"

"Um, sure," she replies in a tight voice.

It's clear she has something she wants to talk to me about. "What is it, Emily?"

"Don't worry about it, Claire and I can handle it. It's nothing," she says, trying to convince me.

"It must be something if you're calling me. What's happening?" There's a long drawn out silence from her end. "Emily!" I snap. "What is it?"

"It's not something we can talk about over the phone." *Fuck.* "I was going to ask you if you can fly out here, but you're hurt, so I'll call Claire and have her meet me where you are. Which hospital are you in?"

"I'm at home."

"You are?"

I nod my head. "Yeah, I am." I lift my hand to touch my chest and wince in pain. "Is everything okay?"

"It's about *work.*"

I thought as much. "I'm home so I'll see you and Claire tomorrow."

"Do you need anything?"

"I'm fine. It's just a flesh wound."

"See you tomorrow." She hangs up and I slide my phone under my leg as I let my head roll back and close my eyes. I find myself drifting in and out of sleep when I hear the front door open. I'm hoping it's Anna, but instead there's a man walking into my house.

"I've been sent by 15," he says. "I'm the nurse." He sets up beside me and checks my vitals.

"Do you have a name?" I ask.

"You can call me Nurse."

Of course I can. "Do you know where 15 is?"

He snorts. "I don't even know how to get in touch with her, so nope," he replies not offering any more.

He's considerably younger than Doctor but just as elusive and secretive. I thoroughly believe even if he did have a way to get in touch with Anna, there's no chance in hell he'd tell me. I guess this is what makes her so dangerous. Her team is fanatically loyal and they all work together like a well-oiled machine. She's at the top, Agent is her second, then she has a team of people who only know what they're supposed to.

Fuck, she's amazing.

I close my eyes as I try to get her out of my mind. But who am I kidding? Anna's made a lasting impression on me. But there's one thing I know for certain. She's gone.

Once I've recovered, I'm going to milk every single contact I have to find her. I don't care what it costs, I want her.

She's mine.

EPILOGUE

ANNA

Months later

"Chief of Police Ben Pearson will now make a statement. No questions." Ben's introduced by a stout-looking woman with long red hair tied back in a severe ponytail. She steps away from the microphone and Ben steps up in his dress uniform.

He looks perfect.

I stare at my laptop screen, focused on him.

Ben nervously clears his throat. "The Bankstown Creek Police Department was given a tip that an abandoned building in the area was being used as a cocaine processing plant. Working jointly with other law enforcement agencies, we executed a coordinated raid on the building." He takes a breath and refers down to his notes. "We had no casualties." He lowers his eyes again, and I can't help but smile at how nervous he is.

"If there was another way, maybe we could've been together," I say to the screen. "Pffft." I roll my eyes and shake my head.

"This drug haul was one of the biggest in our state's history." He looks directly into the camera as the corner of his lip slightly tugs up. "I want to thank everyone involved."

That line always gets me, because with that Mona Lisa smile, I know the cheeky bastard is referring to me.

I close the laptop and lie back on my bed as I think about the months that have passed and just how much I miss him.

No man has ever made me want more, but Ben Pearson did. The problem is *more* isn't something I can ever have. I run the tip of my finger over my lower lip as I recall every moment we spent together.

A part of me wants Ben to move on and be happy, but that part is drowned out by my antihero self who wants Ben to be suffering, just like I am.

My phone rings and I let out a low groan. "Yeah."

"You have a new job."

I look up at the ceiling and blink several times. "Is it time sensitive?"

"No, it's not."

"Where is it?"

"This one is taking you to Germany." I really don't want to go. "And, you'll be super proud of me, 15, I negotiated an extra two million on this one."

"Why?"

"It's a high-profile target."

I purse my lips together and take my earpiece out. Not only did I not want to travel overseas, but I didn't want to kill anyone who's high profile either. I sit up on the edge of the bed and run my fingers through my hair several times as I stare at an invisible spot on the ground.

After several deep breaths, I stand and head into the bathroom. I take a quick shower and dress before leaving my hotel room.

The short drive out to Bankstown Creek gives me enough time reflect on the past few months. Once I killed Lincoln and Natalia, Hunter Inc. fell apart with no one left to lead it. That's given me some relief, although I know when one falls another is always ready to take their place. Thankfully, nearly the entire underworld knows my reputation and what happened to those who ignored it, which means I'm left alone.

I pull up opposite the station and about twenty yards down the street. All I want to do is see him and make sure he's okay. I look down at my phone and stare at the number. My knee bounces as I contemplate dialing it. My lips press together in a tight line as I try to talk myself out of calling him. I close my eyes and breathe for a moment. "Fuck it," I say to myself as I open my eyes and hit dial. My stomach sinks and I feel sick to my very core. What if he doesn't answer?

"Ben Pearson," his silky voice booms. I lean back in my seat and close my eyes. "Ben Pearson," he repeats.

I shouldn't be calling him, not after all this time. "Hi," I say with a quiver in my voice.

"Anna. Where are you?"

I don't answer his question. "How are you?"

I hear him close the door to his office. "Where are you? Are you okay? I tried looking for you."

"No, don't do that." I open my eyes and turn in my seat to look at the station. "I'm doing okay. How about you?"

"Are you kidding? You fucking disappeared and I have no idea how to get in contact with you. Where are you? Can I see you?"

I gulp as I shake my head. "I'm at your house."

"I'll be there in a minute, don't go anywhere."

I hear his chair scraping, then the door opening. "I'll be back later," he says to Grace. I sink down further in the seat but keep watching. "Are you still there?" He bursts through the door and quickly makes his way down to his cruiser.

I allow myself to indulge in a moment of possibility. A small smile tugs at my lips as I watch him from afar. He looks so good. "I'm here," I whisper as he jumps in the car and tears out of the driveway.

"Anna..." he sighs into the phone. "We can make this work."

"In what universe can an assassin and a cop work, Ben?" I close my eyes when his cruiser is out of my sight.

"Look..." Ben pauses and clears his throat. "Promise me you'll stay where you are until I get to you. We have a lot of things to talk about."

I wipe at the tears that are silently falling. "I promise."

Ben must be close to his home now, which means he'll see I'm not there. "There's something I need to tell you."

"I won't go anywhere." My heart hurts as I lie to Ben. He's never going to see me again, it's simply too dangerous for him to be associated with me in any kind of way.

The engine of his car winds down, and I know he's pulling into his street. "You're not here," he says in a small voice. "You left."

"I was never there, Ben. I just wanted to hear your voice." I start my car and pull onto the street. "I wanted to make sure you were okay."

"Don't do this."

"I have to. Goodbye, Ben."

"Anna—"

I hang up before he can say anything else. I rub at my chest as I drive out of Bankstown Creek. Maybe this new job has come at a perfect time. It'll distract me long enough to push Ben out of my mind, and hopefully forget about him.

A light flashes on the dashboard and I'm instantly angry at myself for having to put gas in my car here so close to Bankstown Creek. I've never been so careless in my entire life. Ben could easily drive past and see me.

He wouldn't recognize my car because the one he knew has already been destroyed.

I pull into a nearby gas station and pull up behind a black Volvo. I head in to pay, then back out to the pump. The Asian man from the Volvo is pumping gas and does a double take at me and smiles. Something about him tells me he's not from this area. His hair is impeccably cut and neatly combed back and his expensive tailored suit fits his muscular body perfectly. His black, shiny shoes are probably right for the suit, but here in Bankstown Creek, they don't quite fit in.

"Hey," he says as he looks me over.

"Hey," I respond.

"You heading in or out of Bankstown Creek?"

Wow, talk about being forward. "Out. How about you?"

"I'm heading in. I have some *business* to take care of."

My guard is instantly up. I don't like the way he said that. What business could he have in Bankstown Creek? I click my tongue and shrug impassively. "What a shame, I could've asked you out for coffee, but we're heading in opposite directions."

"Funny, because I was thinking of asking you for a coffee."

"Well, I'll wait for your invitation first," I say coyly. There's something about him that's grating on my nerves. I'm not sure what it is yet, but I'll find out. Other than the fact he looks out of place, there's something else going on.

"Would you like to have a coffee with me?" he asks.

"Do you have time?"

"Everyone from my business meeting will wait for me." How many people are at this business meeting? "Besides," he pauses and casts an eye up and down my body. My skin crawls at his leer, but not because he's unattractive, quite the contrary, he's incredibly easy on the eyes. "Now I feel like coffee." He smirks and arches a brow. "There's a little café down the road that makes good coffee."

"I'm nearly done, so I can meet you down there," I offer. I need to figure out who this man is and what business he's doing here in Bankstown Creek.

"I won't be far behind you."

I finish pumping gas and hop into my car. I take off out of the gas station and head down to the café he was referring to. It's only a matter of minutes before the incredibly attractive man in his fitted suit and expensive shoes pulls his Volvo up beside me. "I can't believe how rude I was," I say as we walk toward each other. "I didn't even tell you my name." I hold my hand out and wait for him to extend his. "Anna Moore."

"Katsuo Vang." He wraps his fingers around mine. The moment our skin makes contact, my heart rate increases as a cold, serpent-like bite quivers through me. The hair on the back of my neck rises and my mind instantly clears and becomes razor focused.

Evil is here.

Bankstown Creek is in trouble.

Ben is in danger.

The job Agent lined up for me will have to wait, or someone else can complete it. I need to find out who this fucker is, and destroy him, because Bankstown Creek and Ben are under my protection.

I don't give a fuck who Katsuo Vang is.

I have work to do.

MARGARET MCHEYZER

Email: hit_149@yahoo.com
info@margaretmcheyzer.com
Facebook: Margaret McHeyzer Author
TikTok: Margaretmcheyzerauthor

Printed in Great Britain
by Amazon